THE GOLD SOLUTION

THE GOLD SOLUTION

Herbert Resnicow

A Joan Kahn BOOK

St. Martin's Press
New York

Library of Congress Cataloging in Publication Data

Resnicow, Herbert.
The Gold solution.

"A Joan Kahn book."
I. Title.
PS3568.E69G6 1983 813'.54 83-9742
ISBN 0-312-33167-3

Copyeditor: Catherine H. Brown

First Edition

10 9 8 7 6 5 4 3 2 1

To Gloria Amoury, who taught me the rules of writing professionally.

THE GOLD SOLUTION

1

"Pearl," I asked, "do you want to kill my husband?"

Pearl has the brownstone next to ours. We used to alternate, but since Alexander got out of the hospital we'd been having our daily coffee and gossip in my kitchen, so I could hear when he got up from his afternoon nap.

"Me? Kill him?" Pearl looked hurt. "I'm trying to save his life, Norma, and yours, too."

"But a murder case?" I protested. "He's never done anything like that before."

"Didn't you tell me to get him more puzzles? Well, this case is a real puzzle."

"I told you to get him books of puzzles, you dimwit. Easy ones."

"Easy ones? For Alex? Are you kidding? He'd know right away."

"I'm deadly serious. He thinks he lost brain cells when he was in cardiac arrest."

"Nonsense. He's just as sharp as he ever was."

"That's what I told him. He got sarcastic. How could a

person of limited intelligence, such as a wife, judge a small change in the abilities of such a superior mind?"

"Can't he tell?"

"How do you know you used to know what you don't know any more?" I replied. "All I need is for him to find one lousy little puzzle he can't solve. He'll blow his top and that will be the end. And what did you do, you dizzy blond?"

"Your husband isn't the only one acting crazy," Pearl retorted. "It's the age; male menopause. Burt has been unbearable ever since I made him take the Talbott case. He is positive he will lose, for the first time in his life. Nina, my niece, calls me twice a day, crying; she will kill herself if her fiancé is convicted. Poor Jonathan is convinced they will bring back the electric chair special for him. Alex is making your life miserable with his frustration tantrums. I thought this would solve all the problems at one time. Alex finds the real killer, regains his confidence, and gets off your back. Jonathan is acquitted and marries Nina. Burt wins the trial and starts acting human again. It was perfect. Perfectly perfect."

Pearl Hanslik is one of those rare beauties, a brown-eyed natural blonde, and really built, but I don't hold her looks against her. She's my best friend, and we do everything together, even though I look like King Kong next to her. She needs me, and I take care of her, because of her handicaps. First, she's badly educated: her Ph.D. is in comparative literature, which doesn't really prepare a girl for life in the Big Apple. Second, she isn't very bright. This is all her husband's fault; Burton never yells at her, not even in private. With this lack of stimulus in the home environment, and an IQ of maybe 145, tops, it's no wonder I have to explain things to her.

"You dum-dum," I explained. "What happens if Alexander doesn't solve the murder?"

"Of course he will. He does a book of puzzles in a day. In ink."

"There's a difference between Double-Crostics and murder. Puzzles are made to be solved, murders are made to be not solved."

"But Alexander always consults for lawyers," Pearl insisted.

"Engineering or construction, yes. Crime, no."

"He solved the Highland Steel case for Burton last year."

"All right, one," I admitted. "But that was white-collar stuff, not murder."

"Crime is crime," Pearl said firmly. "Burton needs all the help he can get."

"But why Alexander? He's in no condition."

"He's our last chance."

"The police are on strike?"

"They've stopped looking. They know Jonathan did it."

"What about private eyes? Burton has to know some."

"Three agencies tried. Zip."

"So what do you expect Alexander to do? Catch the killer barehanded?"

"Certainly not," Pearl answered. "Just solve a puzzle. How could someone, anyone besides Jonathan, have done it? Just the method, not the who or the why or anything."

"I don't know, Pearl. It doesn't sound kosher."

"You have to make up your mind, Norma," she insisted. "Burt will be here any minute, but he will only present the problem to Alex if it's okay with you. Do we play bridge or do we give Alexander a new life?"

"Or do we kill him quicker?" I retorted testily. "Myron

said he had to have three months of absolute rest and quiet. No stress of any kind."

"Do you really think you can keep a man like Alex housebound, helpless, and dependent?" she asked. "Look how he's acting already."

"That's going to stop in a hurry," I told her. "The next time he starts up with me, I am going to bend a crepe pan across his fat skull."

"See? That's what I mean. There is no way Norma Gold, fastest lip on the West Side, can act like a *Woman's Day* wife for three more days, much less three months. Within forty-eight hours, maximum, he will do something Alex-ish, you will open your big mouth and say something Norma-ish, he will explode and he'll get another attack, and this one will kill him, guaranteed. Is that what you want?"

"You make it sound as though it's all my fault, Pearl. Nobody makes Alexander do anything."

"Right. So let him decide. He's a big boy now."

See what I mean about comp lit? Here's a woman who is a year older than I am even though she looks like a teenager, the rat, married for twenty-five years, and she still doesn't know that with men the age doesn't count; that the filthy little beasts grow older, not smarter, or even, you should excuse the expression, more mature.

Just then, the doorbell rang; Burton had arrived. Before answering the door, to make sure I had her full attention, I stood up and loomed over her. In high heels, Pearl is maybe five three, tops. Without shoes, I tower seven inches over Alexander, so I didn't have to loom very hard. "Pearl," I said solemnly, "if I let Burton give this case to Alexander, and Alexander fails to solve the puzzle, he will work himself into such a rage that even nitroglycerine tablets won't help him. If Alexander dies, I will kill myself and you, too. Horribly. Understand?"

"And I'll help you," she agreed. "That's what friends are for. But if he doesn't take the case, he will eat his frustration and fears into himself and die anyway. Not explode, but lose hope, shrink, and wither away. For Alex that would be death by slow torture. Taking the case at least gives him a chance. You must say yes, Norma. You must. Today."

In spite of the heat, Burton was wearing an ascot and a fawn vest under his camel's-hair blazer, making him the best-dressed of the three of us. Every platinum hair on his handsome head was perfectly aligned, and as I bent down to kiss him, I saw he was freshly shaved. He refused iced coffee in the same pear-shaped tones that had swayed a thousand juries, and we went downstairs to Alexander's office on the ground floor.

All 240 pounds of Alexander Magnus Gold were sprawled sloppily across the recliner I bought him when I was finally told that he would get out of the Coronary-Intensive-Care Unit. "Hiya, Burt," he greeted, "caught any ambulances lately?"

"No," answered Burton with mock weariness, "middle-age spread is slowing me down. How are you, Alec?"

"Bored stiff. Myron won't even let me watch wrestling. Too exciting."

"Well, you have to let the old ticker heal a while."

There was a too-obvious silence. Burton's eyes turned slightly, discreetly, questioningly toward me. The question was, really: How do you want to kill your husband? Without consciously deciding, I did what my husband would have wanted, I hope. "Alexander," I said, choking on every word, "Burton has a problem for you."

Alexander brightened and sat up, then looked glum again. "I can't do any expert witnessing yet. Myron won't even let me walk upstairs."

"It's not a construction problem, Alec," Burton said. "I have this murder case I may lose."

"Burton J. Hanslik, world's richest mouthpiece, losing?" Alexander actually smiled. "I thought the moment you walked into a courtroom, the jury voted 'not guilty' and fined the victim's widow."

"Not this time, Alec. And what's worse, it's an internationally famous case. Big headlines: 'Talbott Slain in Locked Studio' and 'Greatest Architect Knifed by Draftsman.' It was only six weeks ago. Remember?"

"I wasn't too interested in other people's deaths at the time," Alexander replied. "So you're defending the murderer?"

"I am representing the poor young man who is wrongfully accused of the crime," said Burton primly.

"Poor? Wrongfully? How will you handle this, Burt?" asked Alexander derisively. "You are so completely inexperienced in dealing with poverty and innocence. How did this poor kid come to you? Doesn't he know what you charge?"

"Well, Pearl suggested—"

"I knew it. Only Pearl could get you to do something this stupid. Did she threaten to withhold her fair white body for two consecutive hours?"

"Worse. She threatened to cook two consecutive meals for me." A base canard. Pearl is the second-best cook on the West Side of New York.

"Will you two clowns stop fooling around?" Pearl was exasperated. "Poor Jonathan is going to be tried for murder."

"Who is this 'poor Jonathan'," asked Alexander, "that you should be so concerned about him?"

"Jonathan Candell is the very sweet boy who is engaged to my niece, Nina Slotkin," she answered. "They met in architectural school. He was a draftsman for Talbott Associates before Roger Allen Talbott was killed."

"How could you let your niece become engaged to a killer," Alexander joked.

"He wasn't a killer when they met," Pearl was not in the mood for jokes. "I mean, he isn't a killer."

"This you know for sure?" Alexander doesn't know when to stop.

"Of course. He's Orthodox."

"Knowing this, the D.A. still had him indicted?"

"He's also a vegetarian," Pearl added.

"The clincher! Burt, get the charges dropped at once. Just tell the D.A. that poor Jonathan is not only engaged to a nice Jewish girl, he is also Orthodox and a vegetarian to boot."

"There are a few little difficulties, Alec," said Burton. "The boy was caught next to the bleeding victim with the bloody murder knife in his hand. No one else could have gotten in or out of Talbott's studio without Jonathan's seeing him. And, to top it all, he cleverly made a full statement to the police without benefit of an attorney."

Alexander scowled. "No money, no guilt, and no brains. A terrific combination."

Burton looked disgusted. "The only thing missing is a movie of the boy slipping the knife into Talbott's back. In Technicolor, with stereophonic sound."

"Just what do you want me to do, Burt?" asked Alexander.

Burton glanced at me uncertainly. I turned away.

Whatever I did now would be wrong. "Figure out how someone else could have done it, Alec," Burton said. He looked at me pleadingly, "He won't even have to leave the ground floor, Norma, he'll just have to think." Back to Alexander, he said, "Give me just enough so I can use the words 'reasonable doubt' to a jury without setting off gales of laughter. It's a classic locked-room puzzle, Alex."

Alex perked up. "Locked-room puzzle? I've never found one that I couldn't solve in five minutes. Tell me about it, Burt, and don't leave out a single detail."

II

Burton began pacing the length of the room, back and forth. His voice took on an address-to-the-jury tone.

"On the day Roger Allen Talbott was murdered, his wife Irma was in the kitchen on the first floor of their brownstone with Linnet Carter, the maid, making up the weekly shopping list. At exactly 10 A.M., as he always did when he was working in his studio on the top floor, Roger called down on the intercom and ordered coffee and an English muffin."

"How do you know it was exactly 10 A.M.?" asked Alexander.

"Talbott was fanatically punctual; he wore an alarm chronometer and he never deviated from his routine. The police reports show that his watch was accurate within five seconds and the kitchen clock was one minute fast. He always had a snack at 10 A.M. and 3 P.M."

"Always coffee and English?" Alexander asked.

"Always hot coffee or tea, even in the summer, with muffin, Danish, or bagel."

Alexander waved Burton to continue. Burton resumed his pacing. "Mrs. Talbott put the food on a tray, pushed the intercom button, and told Roger to release the elevator. When she and Linnet saw the green light go on through the open kitchen door, Mrs. Talbott took the tray to the elevator."

Alexander broke in again, "What do you mean, 'release the elevator'?"

"There is a small hydraulic elevator," replied Burton, "which runs from the cellar to the top floor, with all the controls in Talbott's studio. It is called to a floor by the hall pushbuttons and sent to a floor by the cab buttons, except that it will not go to the top floor, nor will the elevator door or shaft door open at the top floor, unless a fail-safe release switch on Talbott's desk panel is switched on. When this is done, a green light goes on on all hall panels and cab panels to show that the elevator can go to Talbott's studio floor."

"You mean the switch has to be snapped on for each trip to the top floor?"

"It can be left on, but Talbott usually turned it off after each use. He didn't want anyone to come up unless he allowed it; not his wife, Linnet, anyone."

"How did Talbott get up to his studio?" asked Alexander.

"The only way Talbott could get to the top floor was by punching a ten-number routine, which he alone knew, into the combination lock on the control panel in the elevator cab. And that could only be done if he were alone in the cab. If Talbott wanted to carry up more than eighty pounds, or take a visitor to his studio, he would first have to go up alone and release the elevator."

"How did the office get cleaned?" I asked.

"When the regular cleaning crew came, Talbott would let in one man, and watch him until he was done."

"Sounds like an obsessive-compulsive to me," said Pearl, "anal-retentive type."

"Oh, he was crazy, all right," agreed Burton, "but that's expected of a genius."

"What would happen if the electricity failed?" asked Alexander.

"The elevator would not move, and the release switch would spring back to the off position. Talbott could take the stairs down, but he could not go up by elevator until the electricity was restored."

"Why didn't he take the stairs up?" Alexander asked.

"You couldn't take the stairs up to Talbott's office," explained Burton, "only down. The stair is fully enclosed from the third floor to the top floor, with doors at the third and fourth floor. The doors have no hardware on the up side, only panic bolts on the down path."

"What's a panic bolt?" asked Pearl.

"Did you ever see the horizontal bar on a theater fire-exit door?" I asked Pearl. "Pressure on that bar retracts the latch and allows the door to open away from the pressure so that people pushing against the door can get out."

"If that's all," said Alexander smugly, "I don't have to hear the rest. Panic bolts can be opened from the outside if you know how."

"These were," Burton agreed. "Two years ago, a reporter sneaked away from a party and got past both doors into Roger Talbott's office. The next day, Roger had an additional set of panic bolts installed on each door, so that it would take two sets of hands to pick them simultaneously. In addition, he had the bolts wired to turn on red lights and ring bells throughout the house if any of the four latches was not seated perfectly in its strike. He also installed locking-pin hinges and steel plates on each door to cover the latch areas."

"Sounds paranoid," Alexander said. "What was he afraid of?"

"He had some very valuable architectural drawings up there, some valued in five figures. Definitely worth stealing. And he didn't want anyone to see his latest designs."

"There has to be more to it than that, Burt."

"Well, he was very antisocial; went days without speaking to anyone but his wife, and not all that much to her either. Never used a telephone or wrote a letter. Hardly ever went to his office, even. But the triggering event came shortly after he moved to New York. One of my investigators turned it up. Talbott was a dedicated chaser; must have propositioned every blond nymphet in Manhattan. Including, once, the girlfriend of a well-known gangster. The gangster put out a contract on Talbott to break his knees, and then called Talbott to give him the good news, that this time he would be allowed to live. That was when Talbott put in the security arrangements."

"That's the answer," I said. "Get this hood in a cellar and pound on him until he confesses."

"Unfortunately," Burton said, "the hood's business acquaintances eliminated him the week after his Talbott threat, which canceled the contract."

"If Talbott is still fooling around," said Pearl, "there's the motive for his murder."

"If he is," said Burton, "he's doing it very discreetly now. My investigators picked up lots of rumors, but no hard evidence."

Alexander had nothing more to ask, so Burton went on. "Mrs. Talbott took her husband's snack up to him at about 10:08. In about two minutes she returned to the kitchen and continued to work on the shopping list with Linnet Carter."

"At about 10:18, the front doorbell rang. Linnet went to the door. Jonathan Candell was outside on the first-floor landing. He told her who he was and said he had a 10:15 appointment with Mr. Talbott, that he was late, that he had been told that Mr. Talbott gets upset if people aren't on time, and asked Linnet to let him in right away. Linnet had him wait and checked with Mrs. Talbott in the kitchen. Mrs. Talbott said that Candell did have an appointment and told Linnet to announce him."

"Linnet led Jonathan to the elevator, pushed the intercom button next to the elevator, and announced that Candell had arrived. Talbott angrily told Jonathan that he was four and one-half minutes late and—"

"Wait," Alexander broke in. "What were Talbott's exact words?"

Burton's face took on a stern look as he imitated Talbott's words. "Young man, you are exactly four and one-half minutes late. I don't approve of lateness."

"Are you sure those were the exact words?" Alexander's voice was tight.

"Positive," replied Burton. "My staff prepared a summary for me from Jonathan's story, the statements of the other witnesses, the police reports, and their own investigations. We use a private detective agency for all major cases. You think a successful defense is an accident or a Perry Mason ad-lib-in-the-courtroom game?"

"Just wanted to make sure," Alexander muttered.

Burton continued: "Jonathan explained that the subway had been delayed. Talbott asked him if he wanted coffee with a muffin, Danish, or bagel. Jonathan asked if he could have milk and a cheese Danish. Talbott told Linnet to bring up a milk for Jonathan, another coffee for himself, and two cheese Danish. The green light went on, Linnet let Jonathan into the elevator, pushed the fourth-floor button, and went into the kitchen to prepare the coffee. Mrs. Talbott, having heard the conversation through the open kitchen door, had already poured the milk and was getting the pastries, when the intercom squawked. It was Jonathan. 'Quick! Quick!' he screamed. 'Get a doctor. Mr. Talbott's been stabbed!' (Exact words, Alec.)

"Mrs. Talbott shouted to Linnet to get up there quickly and see what was wrong. Mrs. Talbott jumped to the phone and called the family doctor, Dr. Calvin Levin, who, fortunately, was in. He said he would be right over and told his nurse to call a private ambulance at once.

"When Linnet rang for the elevator, the green release light was still on. She took the elevator to the top floor. As she opened the elevator door she saw, through the open vestibule door, Talbott lying on the floor near his work table, blood flowing rapidly from his back and reddening the white carpet. Candell was kneeling behind Talbott with a bloody knife in his right hand. When he saw Linnet, he jumped up and started toward her. Shocked by the blood and by Candell coming at her with the dripping knife, she pulled the elevator door shut and took the elevator down to the first floor. Jonathan was shouting 'Wait! Wait!,' but Linnet wasn't about to get herself killed, too. She tumbled out of the elevator into the arms of Mrs. Talbott, screaming, 'Oh my God! He killed him! He killed him!

"Mrs. Talbott screamed, 'Who? Who? Roger?'

"Linnet was still hysterical. 'He's gonna kill me too! Lemme go. He's gonna kill us all!'

"Just then, Dr. Levin, whose office is on the same block, rang the front doorbell. Mrs. Talbott let go of Linnet and ran to the front door. As the doctor came in, she yelled, "Here. Hurry! Get in." She pushed him into the elevator and pressed the top floor button.

"When they got to the top floor, Dr. Levin rushed into the room, unmindful of his own safety. Jonathan was standing next to Talbott between the body and the table, his hands covered with blood. Levin pushed Jonathan aside, ripped open Talbott's shirt, and pressed a pad to the wound. 'Hold this tight,' he told Irma Talbott. She flinched, then pressed the bloody pad against her husband's back. Levin held a stethoscope against Talbott's chest and listened intently.

"After a few seconds, he put an oxygen mask over Talbott's face and a blanket over his body. He gave Talbott five hundred cc of saline solution intravenously.

"The elevator suddenly went down and came up with two men in white. 'Stab wound in the heart,' yelled Levin. 'Get him to the Trauma Center immediately. I'll call ahead. Give him two units of plasma on the way.' "

"Wait," Alexander interrupted. "How did the medics get in? And how did they know where to go?"

"We checked that," said Burton. "As the doctor and Mrs. Talbott went up in the elevator, Linnet Carter started to run out. She suddenly remembered that she had no money for carfare on her and there was no way she was going to go upstairs to the third floor where her street clothes and bag were. She went back to the kitchen and grabbed a knife to protect herself. She stood nervously in the front vestibule with both the front door and the vestibule door open, so she could run away if the killer came down the stairs or the elevator. When the ambulance crew arrived, she let them into the house and to the elevator.

"The medics strapped Talbott to a stretcher and put him into the elevator vertically. The elevator was so small that only one of them could ride with him.

"Dr. Levin and the other medic ran to the emergency exit door. Levin pushed open the door and ran down the stairs to the floor below. As soon as he touched the bar of the first panic bolt the alarm bells rang and a red light went on at the ceiling opposite the work table. The door swung shut behind him and a few seconds later, the bells rang and the red light flashed again as the door on the third-floor level was opened. On the third floor, Levin found a phone and called the hospital Trauma Center, telling them what to prepare for. He called his nurse and told her to get Talbott's records and to call the Center with blood type and allergy information. He then called the police."

"Why did the doctor go downstairs?" Alexander interrupted "Couldn't he phone from Talbott's studio?"

"Talbott not only didn't use the phone, he didn't allow a phone, TV, or even a radio in his studio. Nothing except the intercom. And that was to be used only when Talbott wanted coffee or in an emergency."

"Short attention span?" Alexander asked.

"He really concentrated on his work," Burton said.

"Sometimes he would stay in his studio for sixteen hours at a time. Got furious if he were interrupted. Had a terrible temper."

"Definitely obsessive-compulsive," Pearl chimed in.

"Anyway," Burton went on, "Dr. Levin realizing that he had left Mrs. Talbott alone with a killer, tried to go upstairs again, but the door had swung shut on its spring hinges. He rang for the elevator and was back on the top floor only a few minutes after he had left the studio.

"Jonathan was sitting on the floor near the knife, looking stunned. Mrs. Talbott was near the elevator vestibule, crying. Levin walked in and said, 'Young man, stand in that corner.'

"Dully, Jonathan obeyed. Levin stationed himself between Jonathan and the knife, making sure not to touch anything. Later, the technical team took photographs, fingerprints, and measurements. There was a clear print of Talbott's thumb on the elevator-release button, unsmudged and at the right angle, and a fairly clear print of Jonathan's right forefinger on the intercom button, overlaying some of Talbott's prints. There were many prints of Mrs. Talbott all over the studio and a few of Linnet Carter's. One set of strange fingerprints proved to belong to one of the regular cleaning-crew workers. Plus, of course, Talbott's fingerprints all over the place. The detective in charge, Lieutenant Joseph Warshafsky, took statements.

"Roger Allen Talbott was pronounced dead on arrival at the hospital. The cause of death was a stab wound in the heart; after the first thrust the knife had been sawed sideways, cutting the heart almost in half. The stab wound had been made by the knife which had been in Jonathan's right hand and which had Jonathan's fingerprints on it."

There was a moment's silence as Burton finished his

performance, then we all applauded, even Alexander. Burton made a half-serious bow, but I could tell he enjoyed the approval. Alexander asked, "Burton, was the problem presented completely? Nothing left out, nothing changed, nothing added?"

"Alec," said Burton proudly, "I have made six-hour summations to juries, giving names, dates, places, quoting witnesses, police reports, medical findings, and things like that. In twenty-five years, I have never been caught in a single mistake. When I take a case, I immerse myself in it; you can be sure that what I told you is absolutely accurate and complete. But if it will make you feel better, I'll give you access to my files."

Alexander nodded, almost absently. When he spoke, his voice sounded far away. "It's not really a locked-room problem; it's an unlocked-room problem. A very interesting puzzle."

Very interesting? Usually Alexander was bursting to blurt out the answer before the other person was finished talking. Alexander spoke again, slowly. "I'll have to think about this, Burt. The solution has not hit me yet."

"You'd better hurry, Alec," said Burton. "The D.A. is pushing for a trial in eight weeks."

"Just before election?" Alexander was surprised. "Is he that sure of a conviction?"

"This is one time I would have liked to be the prosecutor," said Burton ruefully.

Eight weeks? It just struck me! That pear-shaped fop and his sneaky wife had mousetrapped me. I turned on Pearl, "You never told me it had to be solved in eight weeks." I stood up and really told them. "That's it, Burton. You can stop right now. Alexander is not going to work against any deadline; I don't give a damn if poor Jonathan fries or not."

III

Alexander's face paled. He reached into his pocket with his left hand, fumbled a bit, then passed it across his mouth on the side away from the Hansliks. They didn't know what he was doing; I did. Alexander had slipped a nitroglycerin tablet under his tongue to relieve the angina pains that had gripped his heart when I yelled at Pearl. Fast-draw Norma strikes again. Burton and Pearl looked from me to Alexander nervously. Pearl had tears in her eyes.

In a minute, Alexander relaxed visibly. He spoke carefully, quietly, not looking at me. "Send over the files, Burton. I'll think about the problem, but I'm not promising anything. My brain might have been damaged during the attack; I may not be the man I used to be."

"Great," said Burton. "I know you'll enjoy doing this."

"Enjoy?" Alexander looked suspicious. "Do I detect a hint of no fee?"

"The kid's parents have a small candy store in Williamsburg. You want them to sell it? That should net you a big eighty-seven dollars and fifty-three cents."

"That's not what I mean, Burt. My stock in trade is time and talent. That's what I sell to put bread on the table. I haven't earned a penny in the past six weeks. Whatever happens to me, I have to make sure that Norma is taken care of." He looked at me. "How is the bank account holding up, Norma?"

From the day we were married, I've been in charge of the money; Alexander likes it that way. When he has money, he gives it to me; when he needs money, I give it to him. Lately, it's been all outgo. The medical insurance didn't cover a lot of things, and there was no likelihood of Alexander's bringing in very much in the near future. "Getting lower," I responded to his question, "but we'll manage. I got a call from my old boss the other day," carefully not saying who called whom first. "He's desperate, really needs me, waving a huge salary in my face."

Burton looked shocked and said, "I'll be happy to—"

"—lend you a little, temporarily," Pearl broke in, with a worried glance at Alexander. A wife understands the stupidities of macho much better than a husband.

Nobody fools Alexander that easily. Quietly he said, "Tell your old boss, Norma, that your husband is perfectly capable of supporting his wife."

"Alec," Burton recovered quickly, "I really believe you could be the best in the world at this. I will personally pay your standard fee for your work on the Talbott case."

"No," said Alexander firmly. "What I really want just struck me. I want to be a consultant."

"But you are one already," said Pearl. "One of the best in your field."

"I don't want to be a consulting engineer any more," he replied. "I'm going to be a consultant, period. I'll solve puzzles, any kind of problem, on an all-or-nothing basis.

If I succeed, I collect big; if I fail, I get nothing. And I'll eat all the expenses."

All or nothing? With an impossible case like this? Why didn't he ask for a retainer, at least; a guarantee, or even the expenses? No, Alexander the Great, my big-shot husband, has to put it all on the line; not just his life, but the overdraft as well.

"So," said Burton, "solve the first problem. Where is the money coming from?"

"Easy. You have just offered a ten thousand-dollar reward for information leading to the arrest and conviction of whoever killed Talbott, excluding Jonathan."

"Why me? I'm only the lawyer."

"To make Pearl happy; call it a wedding present for her niece. It's a bargain for you. What would it cost you to try this case? Poor Jonathan obviously can't afford even one hour of your time, so no one is paying you anything. And what would it cost in future business if you lost? It would pay your firm to match that amount; talk to your partners."

"You want twenty thousand if you find the killer?"

"Not for a case like this, with an eight-week deadline. I'm taking all the risks and eating all the costs. Can you set it up legally so I collect when I win?"

"In my sleep. What else?"

"Does Talbott have partners?"

"Five. It's a professional corporation."

"Get them to offer a matching reward."

"Why should they?" Burton asked. "They think Candell did it."

"Tell them you have someone who has evidence that Candell is innocent, but won't talk without a reward. If they don't agree, people will think it's because one of them is the killer."

"Okay, I'll set it up. Is it a deal?"

"There's more," Alexander said "Does Talbott's firm carry keyman or widow's-buyout insurance?"

"Both, I'm sure. Why?"

"Insurance companies buy back stolen jewelry at a discount to avoid paying on the claim."

"But the man is dead; they have to pay."

"Not to a killer; a criminal may not benefit from his crime. Make a deal with the insurance companies so I get twenty percent of the money not paid if I prove a beneficiary committed the murder."

"That's big money, Alec. These policies run into the millions."

"You want me to have a strong incentive, or not? Last, go to Talbott's widow and get her to match the firm's reward. Then make a deal with the company that carries Talbott's personal life insurance."

"Just in case the wife did it?"

"Wives have been known to do such things. Other beneficiaries too."

"You could end up with a lot of dough this way."

"If I win," Alexander said, "if I win. I'm fully aware of the odds." He reached out and took my hand. "I know what the life expectancy is for a man of forty-nine who has just had a massive myocardial infarction. I fully intend to beat the statistics, how I don't know, but I may not. And if I don't, I am not going to leave Norma to depend on the kindness of strangers. Or even loving friends like you and Pearl."

Burton looked dubious. "Maybe I was wrong in bringing this case to you, Alec. Even to save poor Jonathan, I'm not sure I want you to take such a risk. You're betting your life against a million dollars. Money, even a million, isn't worth your life."

"It's not that big a risk; I don't intend to shoot it out with anyone, and I don't intend to get excited. And when it comes to puzzles, I'm the best. I don't care how many other detectives are on the case, you can't add IQs. Even if I come in second, Pearl gets her niece married off."

"Well, if you're that determined, all right. You're on the case as of now." Burton leaned back, relaxed.

"Not yet," Alexander said. "There's one more thing I have to do." He got up and walked slowly over to Pearl. Taking both her tiny hands in his huge right paw, he looked deeply into her eyes. "Pearl," he said, "you know that I love you?"

Pearl nodded, slowly.

"You know that I would do anything for you; kill if I had to?" She nodded again.

"But there is one thing I can't do for you. If I find that Jonathan Candell killed Talbott—" He let the words hang in the air.

"I know, Alex," she said softly. "I understand."

"So, as much as I want the job, the money, this new life, I won't take it if there is any possibility that it would hurt you. Tell me again, Pearl. Look into my eyes and tell me again: Did Jonathan Candell kill Roger Talbott?"

Slowly and surely she answered him. "I know that Jonathan did not kill him."

Still looking deeply into Pearl's eyes, Alexander spoke, very quietly. "Pearl, I swear that I will find the real killer. I swear that I will prove Jonathan innocent."

Sometimes I am very proud of my husband.

That feeling lasted a big two seconds. I had news for Alexander. Really terrific news, not that I could tell him. He didn't have to worry about finding the killer in eight weeks.

We had enough money left to keep him in nitro pills and me in Valium for maybe five weeks more, tops.

IV

On West 74th there is a new brass sign: Alexander Magnus Gold Associates, Consultants. Associate Number 1 is a tall dark handsome woman. Dignified, like a duchess; a goddess come to earth. Make that a multigoddess. Mostly Athena the Wise. Obviously Juno from the neck down, as painted by Rubens, who understood what a real woman should look like. A touch of Diana, the Huntress; we *are* looking for a murderer. Too much Hebe, the Cup-Bearer. And a little Venus. Too damned little, of late.

Associate Number 2 is a size-five blond gopher. Pearl was thrilled by the idea of working with Alexander. She thinks it is exciting to be around him (little does she know how much). That it is fun (could be, sometimes). That it is interesting (in the Chinese-curse sense, definitely). And that he is smarter than Burton (he is, by far. Or anyone else, for that matter). That's not strictly true. I outsmart him when it's important. He knows it, too, but lets it lay. He's at least smart enough not to start up with me when he's wrong. Usually.

Pearl does everything I don't: typing, filing, copying,

phone answering, scullerymaiding, slaveying. Basic Gophering. And loving it.

No cooking. She wanted to, but no. Not that she's a bad cook for a blonde, but Alexander must lose weight, and fast; ounce by ounce, the way he put it on. A balanced diet, no sugar or salt, lots of bulk, complete vitamins and minerals; one thousand calories per day, maximum.

Alexander doesn't like the diet. He's discussed this with me three times a day, Alexander style, from the beginning. The very first day home from the hospital, after my practically living next to his bed for a month and gaining six pounds—how do you gain weight eating nothing but Valiums?—my forty-nine-year-old *tsatskeleh* looks me right in the eye and says, "Norma, give me a chocolate bit."

"You've just had three hundred yummy calories," I replied. "That's it. You have to lose weight."

"I do not. Except for a little scar on my left ventricle, I am a perfect physical specimen. Ask anyone at the gym."

"You powerlifters think 'The Hulk' is too skinny. You are five-foot six tall and weight two-forty."

"Solid muscle. I bench press four-sixty."

"Strong fat; you look like a bald gorilla with glasses." This led to further discussion and ended, thank God, in a compromise. He would eat what I eat. Actually, I wouldn't mind losing a few ounces here and there; an eighth of an inch off my waist, a quarter from my hips. Not that he would notice.

Every once in a while, he roars, "Norma!"

In a flash, I am at his side. "You rang, Sire?"

"Get me a full set of clippings on the murder."

"Yes, dear."

"All the metropolitan newspapers."

"Yes, dear."

"In chronological order."

"Yes, dear." I flip on the intercom. "Pearl, bring me the chrono files; papers and periodicals."

He's surprised. "You've done it already?"

"Yes, dear. I knew you would want it." Anytime I'm not ahead of you, buster—

"Set up a cross-reference system; all headings: method, means, opportunity, associates, family, etcetera. You know how to to it, don't you?"

"Yes, dear."

Naturally he doesn't listen. "Take any subject, say the weapon. Make a weapon file. Any mention of the weapon in any context goes into that file, cross-referenced to source."

"Yes, dear."

"If you find any correlations within a file, or between files, flag them."

"Yes, dear." That makes seven times in a row. A Norma Gold World's Record. One more, and he's had it.

"Prepare a complete report on the murder. Objective: Use only witnessed or documented data."

Alexander is sure that no one knows how to do anything without him. I was a top industrial-research librarian for twelve years, with a master's in library science, when we were struggling to establish Alexander's business. It's a great job. Ordering the right material and putting it in the right place is only the beginning. Intelligent cross-referencing is next, which involves figuring out that, ten years from now, someone interested in hybrid vehicles might want to know about the magnetic reluctance of super-cooled gadolinium. For this, you need a built-in crystal ball. Good industrial librarians have them, especially females, who are genetically adapted to anticipating what their lords and masters might want before they want it.

Information retrieval is the best part. It's real detective work, and I'm very good at it. And my husband, who has never used a research tool more complex than an engineering handbook, is telling me how to set up an information system.

One of these days I'm going to let him watch me work. Maybe even help me. Better yet, I'll give him a minor, but troublesome, search to do. Then he'll appreciate my work; maybe even show me a little respect as a professional.

He won't.

Alexander gave me another little job just in case I didn't have enough to do. "I want a full description of the Talbott house. And a set of plans copied from the Building Department. There has to be a way of getting in and out of Talbott's studio that the stupid police haven't figured out yet."

Pearl has already gotten me the police reports and Burton's files. I had gone to the Department of Buildings and ordered a set of the plans of the Talbott brownstone, not just the latest renovation, but the full set, everything, going back to the first filing. I had made careful notes and sketches, in preparation for my report to Alexander. I had been studying the layouts all day, checking one set of sketches against another, trying to figure out a way to commit the murder. No go. At the end, I was trying to figure out a way to break the news to Alexander; there was no way for anyone to get in or out of the murder studio, except for Jonathan. Poor Jonathan.

V

Report: The Talbott House

The Talbott brownstone is twenty-four feet wide and sixty feet deep. There is a fifteen-foot area-way in front, down two steps from the street, which is planted with flowering shrubs; a slate path leads to the downstairs entrance on the right side of the front yard. At the right property line, a set of stone steps leads up from the street to the landing at the formal entrance on the first floor. This landing is supported by a stone enclosure which shields the entrance to the ground floor.

Above the ground floor, which is actually fifteen inches below street level, are three more full floors and the fourth floor, actually an oversized attic behind the steeply backward sloping mansard roofs in the front and back, which is sixteen feet shorter than the other floors.

In the rear, two steps down from the ground

floor, is a twenty-five-feet-deep Japanese garden, surrounded by an eight-foot-high stockade fence.

The windows of the lower three floors are protected, front and back, by exterior wrought iron grilles. The upper floor windows have lighter interior protective gratings.

To enter the house at the ground-floor level, you pass through the unlocked gate in the low wrought-iron fence around the front yard and walk back to the right to the locked iron gate under the first-floor landing. Enter the ground floor through a vestibule which has, typically for the neighborhood, two deadbolts on both the exterior and interior doors.

From the vestibule, the open stairway up to the first floor is immediately on the right. Under the first-floor landing is the door to the enclosed cellar stairs. Just behind the cellar-stair door is a tiny elevator. Continuing along the corridor, some closets on the right and a combination kitchen/bar open to the big game room on the left-rear side of the house. At the far end of the kitchen/bar, against the rear wall of the house, is the vestibule leading out into the rear garden; each door secured with two deadbolts and a sliding bolt.

Starting at the front vestibule again, on the left, across the corridor from the stairs to the first floor, is the door to the wood-paneled library, which is effectively isolated from the game room by a block of six lavatories, three male and three female.

At the bottom of the cellar stairs, against the

front wall of the house, is the electric-meter room. Directly to the right is the gas-meter room, and against the far right side is the boiler room. Under the cellar stairs is a closet, and beyond that, the elevator, with its motor room farther back. Behind the elevator machine room, extending to the rear foundation wall of the house, is a large wine cellar. Opposite the stair is the laundry room. The rest of the cellar is filled with storage rooms.

Visitors enter the Talbott house at the formal entrance, up the front stone stairs at the right side. The vestibule doors, interior and exterior, have vision panels of tempered glass, and are secured by two deadbolts and sliding bolts on each door. Immediately inside the vestibule is a wide hall leading straight to the kitchen at the rear of the house. The double-swing kitchen door is usually left open, so that the maid can see right down the hall to the inside vestibule door.

Entering the hall from the vestibule, immediately to the right, is the landing of the open stairway leading up to the second floor. At the far end of the stair is the landing of the stairway going down to the ground floor. Just past this landing is the elevator. Between the elevator and the kitchen is a large closet.

The left side of the house has the huge living room at the front, which extends two-thirds of the length of the house, back to the dining room. The dining room, which looks out over the Japanese garden, is adjacent to the kitchen; a pair of serving doors connects the two rooms.

There is a pair of large French doors between the

dining room and the living room, and two pairs of French doors between the living room and the hall. When all these doors are thrown open, the first floor, with its wide hall and open stairs leading up and down, becomes, visually and aurally, one big ballroom, with delightful nooks here and there.

The stairway at the second floor, the bedroom floor, is open, too; the master bedroom with its two full baths and two separated dressing rooms takes up the front half of the house. The rear of the house has two guest bedrooms. The second bedroom, on the left, has its own private bath; a guest in the third bedroom must use the bath in the hall, which can also function as an overflow bathroom for very big parties. There are closets in the hall between the elevator and the third bedroom.

The third floor belongs to Irma Talbott. The front of the house is her study and make-up room, complete with theatrically lighted mirrors. In the middle section is a massage room, a sun room, a sauna, a steam room, a hydro-relaxation room with a hot tub and a whirlpool bath, a dressing/locker room, and two lavatories. Across the entire rear of the floor is a gymnasium/dance practice room, complete with barre, mirrored walls, and a piano.

The stairway leading to the top floor is fully enclosed, and the doors at the third and fourth floors have no hardware in the up direction, only panic bolts in the exit direction. These doors can only be opened by someone going down the stairs from the fourth floor, and are wired to flash red lights and ring bells when this is done. At the stair landing there is an iron ladder leading up to the roof scuttle. The scuttle is locked by four sliding bolts. On the roof is an air-conditioning unit.

A small vestibule encloses the elevator at the top floor so that its noise will not disturb Roger Talbott when he is working. Other than a bathroom, the stair enclosure, and the elevator vestibule, Talbott's floor is one huge room, with two small barred windows, front and back.

Centered in the ceiling is a large fixed-dome skylight. Talbott's drafting table is directly under the dome, with a desk at each side of the table. On the left-hand desk is the intercom panel with the elevator-release switch; on the right is a copying machine. There is no telephone. A high draftsman's chair and a small convertible couch complete the furnishings.

The ceiling is covered with white acoustic tile, the floor with white deep-pile carpet. The walls are surfaced with white cork, and the filing cabinets, which line all the walls except the area directly in front of the drafting table, are also white.

Alexander finished reading the report and asked, "Where are the copies of the plans from the Building Department?"

"It takes three days for them to come," I said. "I thought you would like to have this report now."

"Made from memory?"

"No, notes and sketches. Carefully done."

"Any furred-out spaces? Hung ceilings?"

"For a skinny python, yes; for a murderer, no. Also no ducts bigger than eight inches by eight inches. Same for chimney flues."

"Room sizes work out?"

"The police measured. Actual room sizes plus partition thickness equals the house dimensions. There are no false walls, no room for secret passages." He must have really been at a loss if he was looking for such farfetched solutions. "Did you finish reading the description of the murder I put together?"

"A lot of good that did. It was no different from what Burt told us."

"Did you expect him to miss something favorable to Jonathan? The facts are as he told them."

"Maybe," he mused. "Did you get the information only from Burt's files or did you go to the sources?"

"Both," I answered. "Everything in it is verified or corroborated."

"Mostly thirdhand with a bit of secondhand?"

"Forgive your fumbling servant, Sire," I bowed my head. "In the future, when it is time for a murder to be committed in which you may have an interest, I promise to be there in person."

He didn't rise to the baiting, which was bad. "Where's the rest of it?"

"The rest of what?"

"The report of the murder. It's incomplete."

"It is?" I took the report and scanned it. "Ah, yes, Sire, you are right, as always. At the end I forgot to write the name of the murderer."

"Norma—" he growled warningly.

"Have no fear, Sire, I will remedy the oversight at once. The name of the murderer is—" I paused dramatically and looked stealthily over my shoulder.

"What the hell are you doing?"

"Isn't this the point in the movie when a shot rings out from the surrounding darkness and I slump over dead before I can reveal the name of the evil killer?"

"Very funny, Norma. Keep it up. You are going to get creamed."

"The name of the murderer is—Jonathan Candell."

He smiled smugly. "You really think so?"

I didn't like that smile, so I hedged. "Well, the evidence clearly points to him."

"Don't quibble. Did he or didn't he? Talk."

I didn't know whether he had really spotted something or not. Could I have missed it? Or was it his extraordinary ability to see patterns? It's like the follow-the-dots game for little kids; start at dot one, draw the line to dot two, then three, and by dot 147 you have drawn a chicken. Adults can usually look at the dot pattern and make a mental fill-in. Alexander can do it with three dots and a hint. Sometimes less. And fast. He doesn't know how he does it, but afterward, working backwards, he can construct a line of reasoning which could have led to the proper conclusion.

But right now I was in trouble. If I gave the answer demanded by the information, it had to be Jonathan. If I said Jonathan didn't do it, I would have to say how I knew; guessing doesn't count for Alexander, especially with me. Either way, he would lord it over me. He is not a magnanimous winner; I am not a good loser.

So I said, "Did you cheat?"

He looked hurt. "I never cheat. I don't have to."

"What information do you have?"

"Same as you. Jonathan Candell is an Orthodox Jew. He is a vegetarian. Pearl said he didn't do it."

"That's it? That's all? You're guessing?"

"Nope. The pattern isn't there. And Pearl knows people. When she said he didn't do it, she obviously meant that he couldn't do it. If he could not, he did not. Q. E. D."

"That's not enough."

"Plus what you left out of your report of the murder."

"I left nothing out of my report."

"Precisely."

This was very bad. Now he was being mysterious. And paradoxical. That meant he really knew something. He was going to win this one; nothing I could do about it.

"You tell me I left something out of my report. I tell you that I left nothing out. You agree that this is so. Alexander, this is not logical." The ultimate, for him, argument.

"Yes it is." He was smiling broadly. "Perfectly logical."

I didn't see the light. So I said sweetly, as any red-blooded woman would, "Alexander, my love, within the next ten seconds, either I will splinter my best rolling pin on your pointy little head, or you will start explaining. So talk."

By letting him know, through these subtle signals, that I loved him, that there were limits to my patience, that I was not averse to a physical demonstration of both, and that I really did not know the answer, I solved all my problems at one fell swoop.

He talked. "The knife that killed Talbott, what kind was it?"

"I didn't leave out the knife," I protested.

"I didn't say you did. Just answer the question."

"It was an ordinary kitchen knife, the kind you can buy in any store."

"Ahaha!" (Put a crescendo mark over that, with a rising inflection on the last 'ha.')

"What's with the 'ahaha'?" I asked.

"What you just said, 'the kind you could buy in any store.' The murder weapon was not a letter opener or a paper knife or a palette cleaning knife; the kind of knife that would normally be found in a studio."

"That's obvious. You'll find it all in my backup."

"Sure, everything is obvious after I explain it. I don't need your backup, I'll tell *you* about the knife. It is a cheap knife, not a fancy Sabatier. It has a blade at least five, and more likely, six inches long. The handle is between four-and-one-half and five inches long. The blade is stiff, with a sharp point. The handle is smooth and rectangular in cross section, probably plastic. Right?"

"Exactly. How did you know?"

"Obvious. This was a planned murder. Not a mugger off the street who somehow got in and out of a locked room on the fourth floor, bypassing the maid and Mrs. Talbott and her jewelry, who decided to kill Talbott and then left without stealing a thing. I take it, Talbott had money in his pocket?"

"Over two hundred dollars, plus a watch."

"So it was done by someone who knew Talbott and decided to kill him."

"Decided? You're sure, decided?"

"Of course. Premeditated. You think this was a crime of sudden passion by someone who happened to be carrying a big knife in his pocket? And who, in the heat of anger, politely asked Talbott to turn around so he could be stabbed in the back? The killer figured out how to get out of that room under the influence of adrenalin? Or did he plan it?"

"Planned."

"Of course, planned. That's how I knew about the knife."

"How?"

"You're going to kill someone. With a knife—, I'll tell you why later. Do you take an heirloom from your house? One all your friends have seen? It doesn't need your initials on it; all it needs is for Mrs. Talbott to say, 'Oh, I know that knife. It's John T. Killer's favorite carving knife. I recognize it by that funny crack in the jade handle.' And in the crevice between the tang and the handle are traces of rosemary, thyme, and Szechuan red peppercorns, and you are the only killer in New York who uses those spices on Roast Saddle of Lamb à la Killer."

"You're assuming that Talbott was killed by someone he knew well. It ain't necessarily so."

"It is so necessarily so. The kind of thinking and planning required to pull this off had to be done by someone who knew the house, knew Talbott's habits, how Linnet Carter and Mrs. Talbott functioned, everything."

"Okay. Why the knife?"

"Why indeed? Before I go into that, I'll bet there was a knife or some other sharp instrument in the room."

"Two. A scissors and a small knife on his desk."

"So why didn't the killer use one of those? Visualize this: The killer buys a cheap knife in a crowded discount store in a different neighborhood, months ago."

"Agreed. But isn't he taking chances with a cheap knife?"

"No, because he has figured out how to slip it into Talbott's back quietly. There won't be a struggle to bend the blade. I'll bet the autopsy showed Talbott wasn't drugged."

"He wasn't. How did you know the size of the knife? And the shape? The handle?"

"The killer was an amateur. You can kill a man with a four-inch blade, even a three, but to an amateur, it looks too small. He didn't dare let Talbott live after being stabbed; he couldn't take a chance, since Talbott knew him. So he had to have a five-inch blade, which still looks too small, so figure six inches. And for stabbing in the back, it had to be pointed and slim."

"Why not a club or a gun or a rope? Whatever?"

"A gun can be traced; it has to be bought somewhere, from someone. There's another reason, too, I'll come to it later. A club? Not only messy, blood spattered all over the place, but it requires strength to use. Maybe the killer was old, small, a woman. Also a club is unsure. Talbott may have regained consciousness long enough to tell the police the name of the killer. And there's another reason. A rope? Again, skill, strength, and another reason. Poison? Traceable, hard to administer, plus another reason."

"Stop with the mystery already. What's the other reason?"

"Think about the handle of the knife; rectangular in section, smooth, plastic. Why should a killer carry an eleven-inch knife through the streets, take the risk of being seen by Mrs. Talbott or the maid, and figure out a way of getting in and out of a practically locked room, just to stab Talbott? Weren't there more convenient places to kill him? Better times? With less risk?"

"Fingerprints," I glowed. "He wanted Jonathan's fingerprints on the knife. Clearly."

"Precisely." He looked smug. "Not necessarily clearly, but he wanted those prints on the murder weapon."

"And if he knew all about Talbott, he knew that Jonathan would be there at exactly 10:15 that day. But how did he know that Jonathan would pull out the knife?"

"He didn't, but it was likely. Even if Jonathan didn't

touch it, there was Jonathan in a locked room with the man he had just killed and the knife wiped clean of fingerprints. At the very least, it would draw the investigation away from the real killer."

"So all this was done to frame Jonathan?"

"Whether it was Jonathan per Jonathan, or whoever happened to be handy, I don't know yet. But I will, I will. And that's how I know Jonathan is innocent."

"So what did I leave out, even though I didn't leave anything out, wise guy? So far, everything you mentioned is in my report."

"Ha! The three unities of crime. We have opportunity; Jonathan was there. We have the means; the knife. But where's the motive? You left out the motive."

"Because there was no motive, Alexander."

"Ahaha! And hah again! With all your circumstantial evidence, with all your fingerprints and your witnesses, with all your 'no one else could have done its,' you would have me believe that Jonathan Candell, who cannot be a complete idiot, even at his age, bought an eleven-inch knife way in advance, carried it in his clothes to Talbott's house, made an appointment with Talbott in a locked room just so he could kill him at a time and place where no one else could, with two witnesses downstairs, and then carefully left his fingerprints on the knife to make sure he fried for it? You would have me believe he did this with no known motive? For him to want to be caught, yes, *want,* he would have to have a hate so great, or be so crazy, that he would want this murder, and himself as the killer, revealed to the world. So why does he deny his guilt?"

"I don't know, Alexander," I spoke gently. When he is in the state, having completed a complex pattern by sheer exercise of intellect, he is on such a high plane of ecstasy that I dare not shock him, especially in his condition. "Is it not possible, just as conjecture, that Jonathan might have been involved in the murder, and afterwards had a change of heart? Decided not to confess? Due to shock?"

He glared at me. "It's not possible," he shouted. "Jonathan is innocent. The pattern is clear. How can you be so dense?"

I tried to change the subject. "Would you like me to work up a biographical report on Talbott? I could have it ready in two days. Maybe some short reports on his associates?"

"Sure, do that. It will keep you out of the pool halls." At least he was less excited. I had to keep him calm; excitement could trigger another attack.

I could have kicked myself for getting him so upset. Though it wasn't entirely my fault.

I went back to work on the Talbott report.

REPORT: ROGER ALLEN TALBOTT

Roger Allen Talbott, the only child of Walter and Martha Thatcher Talbott, was born forty-five years ago in Washington, Missouri, a small city about twenty five miles west of St. Louis.

Walter Talbott, a big, fat, black-haired man of thirty three, with little education, was a roofer by trade in a time when no one was building. Martha Thatcher was a short, blond, plump girl who married Walter the day after she graduated from high school, because it was better, she thought, than going into a factory. Exactly one year later, Roger was born. Undersized and sickly, the child was sheltered by his mother from the harsh outside world and from his father's contempt.

As a teenager, Roger had no friends and few acquaintances. When he was noticed at all, it was as an insignificant creep.

Roger's grades were a little above passing, except in art, where he got straight A's in every course. He was a natural draftsman who could draw anything he had ever seen in exact and perfect detail. It was said that if three dots were marked on a sheet of paper, he could draw a perfect circle through the dots in one freehand sweep and then put a dot in the exact center of the circle.

At the age of sixteen, he was earning more money than his father, working as an instant-portrait artist at fairs and markets. He had an unusual talent: He would take one look at the model, turn away, and produce an exact likeness in one minute. Like a good son, he gave all his earnings directly to his mother, which did not help relations with his father.

Roger was awarded a special scholarship to the Washington University School of Fine Arts in St. Louis. There it was discovered that he was not an artist. He had no creative talent, and no interest in, or understanding of, composition, color, or light. As a copier, he had no peer; as a creator, he would have failed kindergarten finger painting.

Roger's teachers, the whole department, tried. They wanted, desperately, to bring another Dürer into being, but it was not to be. After three years of blood, sweat, and tears, cosseting and curses, they reluctantly let him go.

Martha Talbott died just after Roger flunked out of school. He blamed himself for his mother's death and, for two weeks after the funeral, worked sixteen hours a day drawing portraits of his mother from memory.

Roger always carried a picture of his mother in his wallet. It was her high-school graduation picture, painted over by Roger in brighter-than-life colors; the hair a brilliant gold, the lips a flashing red, the eyes a bright blue, the skin corpse white.

After a month of mourning he returned to St. Louis, where he worked in a series of advertising agencies, unable to hold a job for more than a year. His skill and speed were appreciated, but his nastiness made him impossible to work with.

It was during an in-between-jobs period, when he was twenty-eight, that he met Irma Miller. She was short, blond, plump with immature baby fat, seventeen, and looked exactly like Roger's mother had when he was an infant. Irma adored him and thought he was the greatest artist who ever lived. With her, not knowing why, Roger was tender, solicitous, protective, and loving. Irma's mother, sensing the sexuality about to burst forth in her young daughter, and appreciative of Roger's sincere affection and his earning capacity, did not object when the couple decided to marry after a six-week courtship.

Mrs. Miller even persuaded Irma's father, a well-to-do hardware merchant, who did not want his daughter to marry so young, to give the newlyweds a house as a wedding present.

Irma asked Roger to design their dream house. In one minute, the story goes, Roger drew a perspective of the now-famous Pyramid House. It may have been that he had just seen a picture of a pyramid on a dollar bill or a pack of Camels; no matter, he could no more help it than he could help breathing. There on the table was a drawing of a pyramid with modern doors and windows, and a chimney poking out of one side.

There are some who say it was an unconscious jab at his father, the roofer: A pyramid has no roof, just walls. Sloped walls, true, but still walls. No building designed by Roger Allen Talbott has ever had a roof in the conventional sense. Displacement murder? Eliminate the roof, eliminate the roofer? Roger's father has been dead for many years; is Roger still killing him symbolically with every plan?

Irma's father thought Roger was crazy, but he was a man of his word. He took his son-in-law's sketch to Thomas Bauer. Commissions were hard to come by, then, for a young architect. Bauer gulped, and made a set of working drawings. Six months later, the house was built.

The local newspaper's cultural critic (part-time) had a half-page to fill. It was a dead period; no visiting opera company, no dance troupe, no book fair, nothing to write about. So no one could blame Wilma (Mrs. Thomas) Bauer for featuring her husband's work. On the other hand, she didn't want potential clients to think her husband was crazy; eastern Missouri was not exactly a center of avant-garde culture in those days. So she took lots of pictures from a low position with a wide-angle lens, wrote a guardedly favorable story, and made sure to note that "the well-known architect, Thomas Bauer, brought to reality the striking design concept of Roger Allen Talbott."

The most prestigious critic of the East's most prestigious newspaper was in St. Louis that day, accepting the honorary degree of Doctor of Architecture from Washington University. The dean mentioned that a very unusual (he cagily did not say "good") building had just been completed by a graduate of the school and another former student of Wash U.

When he saw Wilma Bauer's article, the prestigious critic knew that he had a Sunday feature.

It is at least as hard to be an architecture critic as it is to be a sportswriter. There are a limited number of ways to describe how Team A beat Team B, and they've all been used before. There are a limited number of ways to describe another prismatic office building and *they've* all been used before. But there is one important difference between a sportswriter and an architecture critic. The readers of the sportswriter are more interested in who did what to whom than in counting the number of ways the reporter can say who won. The readers of the architecture reporter however, have, on the average, stayed in school longer, and are therefore more easily bored. And more vocal about it, not necessarily out of an interest in architecture. So where a sportswriter will grasp at novelty, an architecture reporter will snatch at it.

Some lesser critic, one with less integrity and less confidence in the importance of his work in shaping the face of America, might have been content to rewrite Wilma's article in his own inimitable style, but not this one, especially with an honorary doctorate in his pocket. He enlisted a student photographer and went to see for himself. There was, indeed, a story there, the only question was: How to treat it?

Three weeks later, the Sunday supplement featured The Pyramid House, using words like crystalline, seminal, and unshackling. Because anyone can make working drawings, but only geniuses can originate concepts, Talbott was featured as the creator, and Bauer was also mentioned near the end of the article.

If there was a dearth of architectural novelty on the East Coast, there was, that season, a veritable famine in the Midwest. An important Chicago critic, reading his Eastern rival's article, upset at poaching on what was, really, his preserve, and noting that his hated rival had neglected to point out that a pyramid (the Great One, at Gizeh) was one of the Seven Wonders of the World, took advantage of this lapse to produce an article which intimated (it was too early to give unqualified praise; let's see what the West Coast says, first) that Talbott's Pyramid might be considered a Modern Wonder, with the clean, simple, timeless beauty of a Basic Shape enveloping the trite nausea of a tract home.

Another practitioner of the Art of Making Something Out of Nothing (West Coast) realized that his cowardly colleagues had not, as he bravely had, discerned the Birth of a School. Because he had attended architectural school (flunked out, second semester, first year) and the others had not, he knew what to call it in his two-page exegesis of The Front Elevation of The House in a national weekly: The Polyhedral School (not erroneously, although what he had in mind was a regular polyhedron, which a pyramid is not).

Talbott's father-in-law did not get to where he was by being unaware of the benefits of publicity as it relates to merchandising. Having only the best interests of his daughter and her husband at heart, he formed a professional corporation (Roger A. Talbott Associates, P.C.) with his son-in-law holding ninety percent of the stock and the rest divided between Tom Bauer and himself. ("Young architects are a dime a dozen, kid. If I didn't need your license, you wouldn't get even the five percent. Take it or leave it, there are plenty of other hungry registered architects in Missouri who would—") Bauer took it.

In Montana at that time, there was a group of pyramidologists, led by a wealthy retired furniture maker, who believed that the Great Pyramid of Gizeh was the repository of the wisdom of the ages when gods (or extraterrestrials, same thing) walked the Earth, and that the dimensions of the Great Pyramid, properly interpreted, gave valuable information about the past, present, and future of mankind. Pyramids of the right proportions had other astonishing qualities. Dull razor blades placed inside a pyramid became sharp overnight. A steak in a pyramid did not spoil. Sleeping inside a pyramid would increase your life span, obviously.

The Head of this group saw the pictures of the Pyramid House and knew the Ancient Gods had sent him a message. He commissioned Roger A. Talbott Associates, P. C. to design the Great Pyramid of Montana; an exact full-scale replica of the original at Gizeh, but hollow. Inside were living quarters for the faithful, offices, workshops, an auditorium, a library of pyramidology, and everything else needed to facilitate living forever by never having to leave the pyramid. It was Wilma Bauer's idea to provide an interior motel where, for a high fee, senescent agnostics might spend a night with renewed vigor prior to signing over their worldly goods and joining the immortals.

Talbott made a perspective sketch of the building in a minute and turned it over to Bauer. Their retainer was sizable, enabling them to hire a big-enough crew of architects, draftsmen, and secretaries to turn out the job in two months. Bauer was a competent administrator, and the company began to prosper.

The critics who were lucky enough to recognize Talbott's genius before their rivals, wrote up the new venture at great length, not neglecting to mention that they each had been the first to recognize the genius.

This led to several more jobs and another major commission. The Egyptology Department of the School of Archeology of a large Eastern University had just inherited a huge sum from an alumnus who had always envied those fortunate few to whom it was given to grub in malarial areas for potsherds while he was forced to amass millions by arbitraging. The will, drawn by the best unbreakable-will-drawers in Boston, gave the university a simple choice: Build an Egyptological museum, named after the donor, of course, or fight the seven richest charities in America for the right to spend the money (whatever might be left after legal fees) in your own way.

It was clearly imperative to give the commission to Talbott Associates. Roger rose to the occasion.

The stone-faced pyramid was elevated eight feet above grade, supported only in the middle by the mechanical core sheath. It was set in a dished area so you could not see the central support. With strong lights streaming downward, the pyramid gave the appearance of being levitated, supported only on beams of light. The coruscation of the crushed-quartz ground cover and the powerful searchlight beam pointing heavenward from the peak, completed the impression of a pyramidal rocket caught at the moment of takeoff for its return journey to the stars.

On the university's board of trustees were two influential media magnates. Since the project had been brought in for slightly more than double the budget, it was necessary to make clear that it would have been cheap at twice the price, or else the trustees would have been hard pressed to explain the shortage of funds to those junior instructors and financially marginal potential students who were somewhat inconvenienced thereby.

To a media magnate, such problems are no problem. Without a single direct order being given, a flood of worshipful reviews and highly favorable analyses appeared that, while not actually calling for the beatification of Roger Talbott, left no doubt in anyone's mind as to who was the greatest architect of all time.

Irma Talbott's father did not get to where he was by being unable to sense the wave of the future. He had Roger send the original design sketch he had made for each project (autographed and dated) to the critic who had first praised it, noting in his letter (written by his father-in-law and signed by Roger) that no copies existed, that this was the original (for provenance's sake), and that it was in grateful appreciation of that critic's pellucid understanding of what Roger had been trying to communicate as an artist.

Squirrels, worms, and crabgrass know how to make a living. Critics are no less competent in this area, obviously, since otherwise they would have died out long ago. They realized that further good reviews of Talbott buildings, if they appeared early enough (but not before the plans were drawn, one had to be circumspect) would bring in more such small, tax-free tokens of appreciation. The only problem was deciding on the greater benefit; should one sell the drawing immediately (privately, of course) and hang a facsimile next to The Letter (architectural critics, though overpaid, do not have high incomes), or should one hang, and hang on to, the original (for future sale), meanwhile accelerating its monetary appreciation by further building up Talbott designs? (If it worked in the Art Field, why not in Architecture?) There was always the hope that one would be the first to recognize the genius of the next design and thus win another signed token of one's perspicacity. (It was rumored that, three years ago, one of these went for $10,000. Now that Talbott was dead. . . .)

After several small and medium-size commissions, came another big one. The chief executive officer of one of the biggest junk food suppliers in the world, deciding that taxes, potholes, congestion, and muggers were hindering his heavenblest mission to double the dividend, selected Westchester as the perfect location for his new, bigger corporate headquarters. That he had just bought a mansion in nearby Pound Ridge had nothing to do with his decision.

For such a company, there was only one architect. Roger drew two pyramids together, base to base. The lower one was buried, point down, for half its depth in the hard Westchester rock. The building flared outward from ground level to the base of the upper pyramid. From there it sloped back again to the peak, where, surrounded by glass and master of all he surveyed, sat the chief executive officer in his geometrically correct hierarchical position. On the level beneath him was the first echelon of officers; below them, the next level, and so on, to the base of the upper pyramid.

The exposed portion of the lower pyramid contained the service people who made it possible for the uppers to function. In the buried portion of the lower pyramid, the chief executive officer knew, although he did not like to dwell on it, were the disgusting, but necessary, functions of the building.

The only fault the chief found with the building was that there was no button to press that would allow him to deposit the effluent of his private toilet directly on the head of that subordinate who had most displeased him that day. Tom Bauer had to point out that, desirable as the device might be, from the viewpoint of the depositor, at least, the hidebound building codes and health laws of a practically socialist-controlled county limited the methods for intraoffice discipline and sewage disposal.

The building won world-wide acclaim, justifying the decision of the genius who had selected Talbott, even though the dividend was not doubled that year. As a result of that project, Talbott Associates was commissioned to design a skyscraper office building in midtown Manhattan.

Roger, by now, had achieved world-wide fame, and was offered award on top of award at dinner after dinner. Naturally shy and withdrawn, a poor speaker, and lacking social graces, Roger tried to refuse the invitations to these functions and the required afterdinner speeches. His father-in-law insisted that for business reasons Roger must accept every award in person.

They worked out a technique that would save Roger the pain of social intercourse and of public speaking. A large screen and an opaque projector would be set up beforehand. The M.C. would explain that Roger believed in showing rather than telling, and would turn off the lights. Roger would sit at the projector and draw, with his amazing speed, scenes from his childhood, his early work, and his development as an architect, the drawings proceeding in a coherent and accurate pattern. The audience was delighted by the performance, and showed its approval by sustained applause. When questions were asked afterwards, Talbott would answer immediately with another quick drawing or two. As Roger gained experience in this technique, he would often go through an entire evening of ceremony without saying a single word, letting his pencil speak for him.

It was clear to Irma's father, who did not get to where he was by not knowing when the time had come to pull up stakes and head for greener pastures, that the firm had to move to New York, where the money was. It was also clear that the firm had to expand, since two more big, prestigious commissions had come in: one from the Bayerischer Rundfunk, the Bavarian State Radio Network, and the other from the Mozarteum, in Salzburg.

It would have been no problem for Roger to sketch all three pyramids right away. The trouble was that the Europeans required Roger's presence, both in Munich and in Salzburg, under the impression that Roger needed to see the site and to discuss the design program.

Roger did not want to go to Europe, or to talk architecture with clients, but Irma, who still looked like Roger's young mother, won him over by pouting and begging, and pointing out all the wonderful new things he could sketch there.

The firm's stockholders were expanded to include two of the senior staff members, John Bishop and Francis Dakin, plus Erik Kirsch, a young designer of great promise. Bauer and Dakin would stay behind to complete the work of the St. Louis office and Irma's father would devote full time to the financial administration and prepare for the move to New York.

Bishop was to stay on in Salzburg to conclude the design program with the owners after Roger made his presence felt, and then go to New York to set up the new office. In the same way, Kirsch would stay on in Munich after Roger and Irma returned to New York. After Dakin and Bauer completed the work of the old office, they would join Bishop in New York, where all new work would be done, starting with the office building.

Roger grew bored with the discussion, leaving Irma, her father, and the other four partners to make the decisions. He sat at a drafting table and quickly sketched the office building. It was a square-sectioned, smooth, metal-clad tower, going straight up for fifty-three stories, with a pyramid at the top, bare and graceless, unlike the Washington Monument which, except for the taper, it resembled.

(The critics went wild. "Talbott has not pandered to the masses by tapering the sides, he has not made obeisance to entasis, the mentality of the past; this is not a slope-sided obelisk or a menhir. It is a clear, sharp, revolutionary statement which says, 'here is a new age, bare, honest, geometric. Train your eyes to see anew.' And for a fillip of humor, of contrast, to show the new raising the old to the heavens, he has blazoned his trademark at the top.")

Roger went back to the conference room, slapped the drawing down in front of Bauer, and left. Bauer was upset and started to go after Talbott. Irma's father gently stopped him, reminding him that every one of Roger's designs had looked no better than this at first, and that each had been praised and earned the firm lots of money.

A few minutes later Roger walked in again. In front of Kirsch he laid the sketch for the Bavarian Radio and Broadcast Tower, a highly elongated pyramid reaching two hundred meters in the air. The lines were angled straight from the fifty-meter-square base almost to the tip, to the point where the cross section was ten meters square. At that point the edges of the narrow pyramid grew vertical, forming an inner cube ten meters on a side, from each side of which a pyramid thrust out horizontally, pointing north, south, east, and west, like electrodes discharging energy to the four cardinal directions. A fifth pyramid topped the spire. Jokers later called it the Bavarian Morningstar, after the weapon used by head-bashing Teutonic knights.

In front of Bishop Roger placed the sketch of the Salzburg Everyman Outdoor Playhouse. This was an inverted pyramid, like the bottom half of the corporate headquarters in Westchester, with the apex sunk in the ground. Grecian amphitheater-like step-seats were cast in place along the inside walls of the hollow inverted pyramid. The ancient drama could be played all over the theater; in the center, along a step-seat row, up and down the radial lines of the terracing, or along the top edge of the inverted base where the narrow walk, without guardrails, heightened the tension of the audience and the players outlined against the sky.

Bishop took the drawing—stunned.

Four months later, Bauer leased one floor of a large office building, bought furniture, hired people, and set up the office. Roger's father-in-law bought, for Roger and Irma, the East Side brownstone in which Roger Allen Talbott was to be murdered eight years later.

Irma Talbott was delighted with the town house. Within a long walk or a short ride was the greatest concentration of cultural activities in the world. And when Irma discovered The New School, that almost endless source of culture, soft science, and personal growth, her cup ran over.

She had always felt that she was a natural-born decorator and redesigned the interior of the brownstone herself. Even Tom Bauer, who had the pleasure of producing the working drawings, had to admit that her designs were, if you liked the ultra-modern, equal to the work of many of the professional interior decorators he had worked with.

The only area she asked anyone about was the top

floor, Roger's studio. He told her what he wanted, and she produced it, exactly. At the housewarming, when toasts and compliments flowed, the world's greatest architect publicly acknowledged his wife's skill and talent, and thanked her for making a perfect place for him to work, before he disappeared upstairs.

Irma Talbott took to wealth easily and unostentatiously. She did what she wanted and spent what she wanted, but never rubbed anyone's nose in her money, nor did she snub the poor, the unlucky, or the as-yet-unrisen artist. Her friends and acquaintances (Roger had none) ranged from starving artists, actors, and students, whom she quietly fed and helped up the ladder, to the greats of the world. Her salons and soirées were internationally famous, and her home was sometimes requisitioned for charities or political causes. Roger, shy and reclusive, would, when he was home, make a duty appearance at each gathering and, when he wearied of the fawning and the flattery, would retreat to the peace of his workroom. Amid the brilliance of the swirling fauna and flora of his wife's life, the absence of his drabness went unnoticed.

In death, he left a dark red blot on a pure-white carpet.

VII

Alexander laid the report down disdainfully. "What kind of crap is this?" he asked.

"The very best kind of crap, darling," I answered respectfully. "What kind of crap did you want?"

"Don't be cute with me, Norma. You were supposed to give me a package of data. Objective. With full backup. Instead I get a dozen pages of opinion, guesswork, fantasy, and editorializing, complete with your smartass snidery."

"That is a perfectly objective abstract of the subjective information available."

"I must have facts; raw data."

"Life doesn't work that way. You want to find the killer, find out how people feel."

"First I have to find out who benefits from Talbott's death. That I can get from the data."

"Lots of people benefit from Talbott's death. Other architects, for example. Even you may benefit, if you open your mind a little."

"You're telling me I'm a suspect? And the entire membership of the American Institute of Architects?"

"I'm telling you that benefit may not be enough. Some people may kill even when it doesn't benefit them, if the hate is strong enough."

As usual, when he's losing, he changed the subject. I don't mind; it shows he understands my point. "How did you get this information together so quickly?"

"Pearl was up half the night typing. Later, tell her how much you appreciate it."

"I mean the information."

"I have my methods, Watson."

He pinkened. "Role reversal, darling? The Baker Street Irregular has ambitions above her station? Just remember who is the retained consultant on this case."

"I remember, O Master, and I have just decided that Assistant Drudge is not a fit position for a Nice Jewish Girl like me. So go gather your own information. Excuse me, data. And file it in the appropriate orifice."

"Norma, you're taking unfair advantage of me. You know I can't even leave the house for another week."

"True."

"We would make a lot of money out of this if I succeed."

"So succeed. Who's stopping you?"

"I can't do it without you."

"Aha!"

"So what do you want me to do?"

"Try saying 'we.' "

"We?"

"As in 'if *we* succeed.' "

"Very well, if you insist."

"In front of Burton too."

"Burton?" I nodded. "All right," he said, "but only Burton."

You have to know when to stop. A completely crushed ego is not very good in bed. On the other hand, you do have to give the filthy little beasts a touch of the whip, on occasion. As a reminder. To keep things from getting completely out of hand.

"How accurate is the report?" he asked.

"Very, I think."

"Backup material?"

"The copies of the birth certificates, diplomas, awards, all that stuff will be here in a week. You need assurance he was born?"

"I need to check the data against the information. If there are any holes, inconsistencies, patterns, it may lead to the killer."

"My abstract is very accurate. The backup will show who told me what. Everything I gave you is corroborated."

"How could you have checked all this out in two days?"

"I'm a librarian, remember? Research type? For me, this is child's play. I called the public library in Washington, Missouri. And the Chamber of Commerce, the City Clerk's office, Wash U. in Saint Louis, teachers, friends, relatives, neighbors, everybody. And I made a deal with a reporter on the *Post-Dispatch.*"

"What kind of deal?"

"When we find the killer, he gets an exclusive."

"Fair enough."

"I also made the same deal with the *Times,* the *Post,* and a few other papers."

"That's dishonest!"

"Of course, darling and it's all for you. I told each librarian I spoke to that you would personally call her as soon as you found the killer. There's nothing a librarian loves as much as getting the information straight from the horse's mouth."

"My God, everyone in the world will know that I'm—we're working on the case."

"Of course, darling." I gave him a "smart doggie" look. "That will make the killer so nervous he'll make a mistake and then we'll nab him."

"Yeah? What if he is so frightened of me that he decides to bomb the house?"

"Darling," I hesitated. This had to be put very carefully. "I know it, and you know it, and our small circle of friends knows it, but I don't think everyone knows that you are one of the most brilliant men in the world."

He bridled. "One of?"

"Well, darling, there's me, at least."

He definitely reddened and his voice got louder. "I have the highest recorded— You are not— Eight points in significant— You lied!" He tried to get so many words out at once that I thought he'd choke.

He was referring to the time he decided to join Mensa. He wanted me to join too; he hates doing anything without me. Which is one of the reasons I haven't left him. Yet. When I told him that having an IQ in the top two percent of the population was not my only requisite for choosing friends, he accused me of being afraid of taking the test.

I told him that what I was really afraid of was the effect of his ego when he saw how much higher I scored than he did. After what one might call a heated discussion, I agreed to take the test after his score was computed, so that I could be sure to score exactly eight points lower than he did, like a dutiful wife. He laughed on the other side of his face when that was exactly what I did.

He was furious, accusing me of lying when I told him what I would do. I wasn't really lying; it was just a normal wifely precaution. Had I scored, say, twelve points less, I would have explained that, at the last moment, I decided that eight points was too close for proper wifely humility and decided on twelve as being more appropriate. And, of course, if I hit eight points exactly, I had him cold. What could I lose? Any wife would have understood.

"You lied!" he screamed when the scores came out. "No one could pick the exact score on an unfamiliar IQ test. It's inconceivable. Do you know what kind of IQ a person would have to have to produce an *exact* score at that level? Do you?"

"Of course I know, darling," I answered, "I did it. I understand why you can't conceive it, at your level, and I sympathize. But it's all right, darling, I promise not to tell anyone if you won't. And if you ever have a problem, just come to me. I'll always be around to help."

He's a man, and therefore, glandularly, a square. And so sure of his ability, it would never occur to him to cheat. Which is why I'll always be ahead of him. Which makes me really smarter. Except in certain technical matters. Which don't really count. Unfamiliar IQ test? Whatever gave him that idea? I'm a research librarian, remember? Nothing that is recorded can be unfamiliar to me. Nothing.

He changed the subject again. Twice in one conversation, he admitted, in his own way, that he could not win. A record.

He thought for a moment, then said, "Bring Jonathan here. I want to check a few things. Don't forget, my job is only half done. I've proved him innocent," his eyes challenged me, "but to get the rewards I have to provide information leading to the arrest and conviction of the real killer." Then, as an afterthought, he added, "And darling, thanks for all your help."

I hadn't forgotten about the money, really. I kissed him gently. Could I tell him that I had already arranged to have Jonathan here tomorrow? No. If I got too visibly far ahead of him, I might get a Stakhanovite Medal for Efficiency pinned to the divorce papers. Divorce is too important to be left to husbands; if we ever get divorced, I'll be the one who decides.

We won't. He thanked me just now. He's learning. It's taken twenty-seven years, but he's learning. Who knows how much more he'll learn in the next twenty-seven?

I hope.

"Today," I announced, "you can go for a walk." Myron had checked Alexander the day before and was pleased with his weight loss and rate of recovery. "I don't care how good you feel," I warned, "you walk one-quarter mile, no more. At a slow pace. Enjoy the sights. Don't breath the car fumes." I kissed him and adjusted his sunhat.

Pearl walked in and looked surprised. Hammed it up a little, but he didn't notice. Or didn't mind. Because she's tiny, blonde, and beautiful. If I were to step out of line one inch, the screaming would be heard in Canarsie. "Going for a walk, Alex?" she asked. "Can I go with you?"

Of course he said yes, I don't think any man has said no to Pearl since she was two. Probably not even then. But at least I had someone to walk with Alexander, just in case. Good recovery sounds fine, but from where was the recovery? So if you think I was going to let him go out solo on his first day, you are sorely mistaken. I could just see him lying on the sidewalk, unable to move, with people carefully stepping around him.

Naturally I couldn't go. God forbid I should even suggest it. I can hear it now: "Am I a baby that I need a nursemaid to go outside? You think Alexander Magnus Gold needs a woman to protect him? You're trying to run my life."

No, Alexander, not run your life. Shield your life, that's all I want. To keep you alive and make you happy. I don't want to be one of those Florida widows. My only wish is that we go together when we have to. In spite of your complaints, I know how much you love me and need me. And I couldn't live without you; I wouldn't want to. That's why I sent Pearl with you today. And every day. She'll be pleasant company. She'll show you how to look at life with new eyes; maybe you'll learn how beautiful life is. Maybe, now that you've been dead, and are still so close, so weak, so vulnerable, maybe now you'll learn to appreciate what you have, including me. Maybe, even, be a little more demonstrably affectionate and loving, even in public. It's not to be ashamed of, to show how much you love your wife. You like it when I do it.

That's why I'm sending Pearl along with you. While

you build up the supplementary blood vessels on your heart, she'll build up your ego, because she really likes you and admires you. She'll protect you and help you if, God forbid, you get another attack when you're away from me. She'll watch over you, and she'll watch you too, to make sure you don't drop in to the Hungarian Bakery on the corner. Because I know what a sneaky, weak-willed rat you are. You would rather eat a Dobosch Torte than live twenty years more with me. And I won't let you kill yourself, even if you hate me for it now. Why couldn't I have loved a normal man?

I had timed it so Alexander would have a half-hour nap on the recliner before the meeting with Jonathan. There were no crumbs on his shirt. It's not that he's stupid, he just thinks he eats neatly. I trust Pearl, but like all women, she's very motherly when it comes to Alexander. I told her that if I find so much as one M&M in her bag while she's working here, she gets a week's banishment.

At exactly eleven o'clock, Burton brought in Jonathan. He was a slim young man of average height, hair a nothing brown, as were his eyes. His pale complexion showed he was an indoor type. What a nice girl like Pearl's niece saw in him, I could not imagine. Love is not only blind, love is dopey. When I first met Alexander, he was poor and short, but he had something special. He was a man at twenty-two; Jonathan is a boy at twenty-four.

I put the tape recorder in the desk drawer, with only the microphone out. People talk differently when they're being recorded, so I don't flaunt the machinery. Pearl doesn't take shorthand, my usually perfect memory is not perfectly perfect, and, since Alexander's memory is nowhere as good as he thinks, a tape recorder saves disputation; it being a lot harder to call a recorder a prejudiced moron than a wife.

Burton the Attorney wanted the recorder off. Alexander was irritated. "Look, Counsellor," he said, "I'm supposed to help Jonathan. I'm not working for you; I'm not even working for Jonathan. I'm freelance, remember? I know he's innocent," he looked at me meaningfully, "but I have to talk to him freely. That means without you. I can't function if you are going to make objections. So please, Burton, leave."

Burton Hanslik, Defense Counsel Supreme, was about to have a stroke. "Do you realize," he fumed, "that what he tells you is not privileged? You want me to leave my client unrepresented?" He made it sound like flayed.

Pearl looked at him and said, "Please?"

Burton left. She says "please," and her husband abandons his judgment, his professional ethics, his client, and his senses. I have to practically grovel to get my husband to take me to a serious foreign movie. Someday I'm going to dye my hair. Blond, I mean.

Alexander turned to Jonathan. "Why did you go to Talbott's house?"

"Mr. Miller told me to."

"When? Exactly what did he say?"

"He said, this was Thursday before lunch, that Mr. Talbott wanted to see me at his home on Sunday at exactly ten-fifteen. And to be on time."

"Why didn't Talbott meet with you at the office?"

"Maybe he wanted to talk to me unofficially. He hardly ever came to the office."

"Did you ever talk to him before?"

"No. The only time I saw him, he was walking through the office with Mr. Bauer."

"Why were you late for the appointment?"

"I left fifteen minutes early to make sure. The subway was delayed. Even so, I was only two minutes late."

"How do you know that?"

"When I rang the bell I looked at my watch. I had set it by the radio that morning. The maid opened the door and I told her I had an appointment. She made me wait outside before she let me in."

"How long did that take?"

"About a minute. She took me to the elevator and spoke to Mr. Talbott on the intercom. He was upset that I was late, but he told me to come up and told the maid to get me milk and a cheese Danish."

"Wasn't there something about releasing the elevator?"

Jonathan nodded. "He said he would release it. A green light went on and she pushed the top button and I went up."

"How long did that take?"

"Less than a minute. When the elevator door opened I was in a small vestibule. I pushed open the door—"

"Wait. You say pushed? Wasn't the door shut? Latched?'"

"It was almost closed, not completely. I saw Mr. Talbott seated near his drafting table with—"

"Was he alive then?" Alexander leaned forward, tense.

"Yes. He had the knife in his back but at first it didn't register. I took a couple of steps into the room, it was very quiet, thick carpets, and I didn't think he knew I was there, so I said, 'Mr. Talbott?' and he turned around and pointed at me."

'With his finger?"

"He swiveled left and pointed his left hand at me. Then I saw the knife."

"Why didn't you see it before?"

"There was very little blood at first. Then he fell off the chair sideways."

"Did he say anything?"

"He made a sort of choking sound. By then I was at the desk and I saw the intercom. I pushed the main button and yelled that he had been stabbed. There was no telephone."

"How did you know which button to push?"

"They were labeled. I pushed the one marked 'all.' "

"Talbott was still alive then?"

"Yes. He was trying to roll over. I went back to him."

"Back? Where was he lying?"

"Next to his chair, a few feet back from the table. Without thinking, I pulled the knife out. The blood gushed out on the carpet."

"With your right hand? Are you right-handed?"

"Yes. Then I took my handkerchief and tried to stop the blood. The elevator came up and the maid came in. She took one look and started screaming. I stood up and said, 'Wait, wait,' but she jumped back into the elevator."

"Talbott was still alive then?"

"I think so."

"How long before the doctor came?"

"A couple of minutes. He started to work on Mr. Talbott right away."

"Did you hear any bells? See red lights flash?"

"You mean the emergency exit? Mr. Hanslik told me about that. Only when the doctor opened the door."

"You told all this to the police?"

"Why not? I had nothing to hide."

"Innocence is no excuse." Alexander looked at him unbelievingly. "You should have kept your mouth shut."

"I did not kill Mr. Talbott. Everything I told the police was the truth. Maybe it will help them find the real killer."

"They think they already have. And nothing you told

me would make anyone think otherwise. Let's try another tack. What reason would you have to kill Roger Talbott?"

"I could not kill anyone. It's against my religion."

"If a Nazi were attacking your mother? You wife? Your children? Your rabbi?"

Jonathan was silent. Alexander pressed him. "Come now, Jonathan, would you kill under those circumstances?"

"If there were no other way, to save a life, it is possible. But first I would try to restrain the other person, to reason with him."

Alexander looked at me; I knew that look well. The day before, on TV, a social sciences type had insisted that what the world needed—no, not the world, just the United States—was *forced* equality. Alexander had looked at me that way then.

"And if reason failed, Jonathan?"

Jonathan remained silent. Alexander kept pressing. "So we know you might kill, given the right motive. What motive could you have had for killing Talbott?"

"None." Jonathan clamped his mouth shut stubbornly.

"So short, so curt," Alexander taunted. "And Talbott invited you to his home on a weekend just for coffee and Danish? What relationship did you have with him?"

"Mr. Miller just told me to go there. He didn't tell me anything else. Go ask him."

"I don't have to, I'm asking you." Jonathan pressed his lips tightly together. Pearl was ready to jump up and tell Alexander to stop pressuring the poor sensitive boy. Alexander does not take kindly to having a chain of logic interrupted, or a pattern of Socratic discourse. The least we could expect would be a history of interruptions, a lecture on the obstruction of learning and the destruction of knowledge, starting with the Person from Porlock, through irreplaceable manuscripts thrown into the fireplace, to the burning of the library at Alexandria. Plus a week of pouting, a complete withdrawal from the case, and a possible heart attack. If Pearl opened her mouth, she could have sensitived Jonathan right into a twenty-five-to-life.

So I put my hand lightly over her mouth and whispered, "Shut up, or I'll tell."

While she was trying to figure out how I knew, what it was, and to whom I would tell it, the moment of danger passed.

Alexander went on, "Jonathan, I am going to give you, for free, a Gold's Law: There are two four-letter sources for ninety percent of all human troubles: S-E-X-X and M-U-N-Y. In your case, let me start by describing your fiancée, Nina Slotkin, whom I have never seen, not even a picture. She is short, blond, blue-eyed, slightly plump, and looks like a teenager. Right?" Jonathan turned red and held his lips together even more tightly.

Alexander smiled smugly, "I thought so. That being the case, she has to have been, somehow, in contact with Roger Talbott. Since you met her in architectural school, she may have been a summer replacement draftsman for Talbott Associates."

"You're wrong," shouted Jonathan, "you don't know anything. Nina couldn't get a job as a draftsman. She works in an art-supply store."

"Thank you, Jonathan," said Alexander. "Where she works doesn't matter. What is important is that Roger met her, took a liking to her, and, to be old-fashioned, has been trying to force his attentions on her."

"No! She never—" Jonathan was very upset. "Nina is not— We never even— She's a nice—"

"I'm sure she is," Alexander interrupted, "but Talbott persisted, didn't he? You found out. This enraged you, the thought that he was trying to seduce your intended wife."

"I didn't. I couldn't. All I wanted was—" He stopped suddenly.

"Of course you didn't. And couldn't. And wouldn't. Not for a little thing like another man pursuing your fiancée. Or even raping your fiancée. But would a jury believe that?"

"It's the truth." Jonathan was very pale.

"And it's also clear that Talbott didn't send for you to discuss the girl. He probably didn't even know she was engaged to one of his employees, not that it would have made any difference to him. So we come to that other great driving force of human civilization, money. He sent for you, a lowly draftsman, to discuss money. Let's analyze that. Let's see if you, who would not kill for love or money, would kill for love *and* money."

Jonathan stood up, trembling and stammering. "You're not on my side. You're trying to get me sent back to jail. Nobody knew about Nina or . . . or anything. She didn't have anything to do with this. I didn't want to get her involved so I never told anyone about her . . . him . . . them. Not even Mr. Hanslik. Now they're going to think I had a reason to kill him. And I didn't. I really didn't." He turned and ran out.

Alexander was pleased. "Well," he said, "now we're getting somewhere."

Pearl was confused and hurt. "Alex," she asked, "why did you do this? You've upset him terribly. And you've found a possible motive, not that I think so, for him to have killed Talbott."

"Take it easy, Pearl," he soothed. "Anything I discovered would have come out eventually, maybe at a worse time. And I found a motive for Jonathan, imagine what I might find out about other people when I dig further."

"But this is terrible," Pearl was shaking. "Burton will . . . he gets furious when clients don't tell him everything. He might even drop Jonathan."

"So don't tell him," I said. "And if you're a good little girl, I won't tell him either." She didn't laugh.

"Of course we'll tell Burton," Alexander said, "but at a more propitious time."

I changed the subject quickly, before Pearl had time to get hysterical over Alexander's clumsiness. "What made you think that Nina Slotkin was involved?" I asked. "And how did you know she was blond and blue-eyed? Pure guesswork?"

"Of course not," he answered. "It was obvious. As I said before, sex and money, the two major motivations. The millionaire boss of a company is not going to discuss money matters with a poor, very junior employee, especially not on a weekend. I only threw that in so Jonathan would deny it and be forced to zero in on the sex angle. And given Talbott's paranoia, he would certainly not invite the kid into his sealed vault of a studio for some trivial thing such as a ten-dollar raise. So it had to be sex. If Talbott liked boys, it isn't in his report, which I take to be accurate . . .", he looked at me questioningly and I nodded reassuringly, ". . . and if he did like boys, surely he wouldn't fool around in his own home with the maid and his wife there. So it had to be Jonathan's fiancée. As to her looks, there's Talbott's obsession with his teenaged blond mother, his choice of a teenaged blond wife—it was in your report, Norma—his chasing blond nymphets. So who should Nina look like, Talbott's father?"

"You're right, Alexander, it was obvious," I tried to keep the sarcasm out of my voice. But guaranteed, there had to be some guesswork involved; the logic came later.

"Interview Talbott's father-in-law, Miller," he said to me. "Find out why he set up that appointment with Roger for Jonathan."

It wasn't just politeness that kept me from reminding him of his brilliant deduction that Jonathan Candell was not the murderer because he had no motive.

IX

Pearl was going stir crazy. It finally having sunk into her little blond brain that gophering is not the highest calling of mankind, she insisted on going detecting with me. Alexander, by now, was allowed to walk upstairs, so I let her come along. Besides, Bloomingdale's was on the way to Miller's apartment, so we could sneak in a quick hour of shopping.

Rufus Cornelius ("call me R.C.") Miller was a plump little man with a fringe of white hair all around his head. He would have looked like a beardless Santa Claus if his bright blue eyes were a little less sharp.

R.C. apologized for the quality of the coffee he insisted on making for us. Wanda would have done much better, but she was chairing a meeting of the Mayor's Committee on Aging that morning.

Having Pearl along was a big plus. It wasn't that a man was unwilling to lie in her presence, but with all his glands concentrating on her, he couldn't be bothered with minor things like concealing evidence. R.C. couldn't take his eyes off her; eight to eighty, they're all alike.

"Yes," said R.C., staring into Pearl's soft brown eyes, "I told Candell to go to Roger's office."

"Did you confirm this with Roger?" I asked.

"No, with my daughter, Irma. She takes care of Roger's schedule when he's at home."

"But Roger knew about it?"

"I had discussed it with him the week before. He didn't particularly want to meet the boy, but I convinced him it was our only chance."

"Only chance to what?" This sounded like a break.

"Didn't Candell tell you?" R.C. was being cagey. "Maybe he didn't want his motive for killing Roger known."

"I'd prefer to have your side of it," I said casually.

He tore his eyes away from Pearl. "Mrs. Gold, there is no my side. The fact is that Candell was caught with the knife in his hand seconds after Roger was stabbed. Even he doesn't claim that anyone else was there."

Pearl spoke softly, "Jonathan didn't kill anyone. He couldn't."

R.C.'s voice softened, too. "Mrs. Hanslik, I understand how you feel. When I met the young man I got the same feeling you did; that he was a namby-pamby who wouldn't life a finger to save his own life. But I have lived long enough to know that, given the right provocation, even a mouse will kill."

"Do you believe there was sufficient provocation for Jonathan to kill Talbott?" I asked.

"I didn't say that. There wasn't any reason for Candell to kill Roger; more like the other way around. Unless there is something I don't know about." He looked at me shrewdly.

I wasn't about to mention Nina to anyone, much less Roger's father-in-law. Instead I said, "What do you mean, the other way around? Did Roger have any reason to kill Jonathan?"

"Certainly not, just a business problem that could have been settled in a business-like way."

"Talk straight, R.C., no phumpha-ing." I was firm.

"Well, I suppose you could get it from your client." He hesitated for a moment, then spoke. "Talbott Associates is a very profitable firm in terms of net versus volume. We're nowhere as big as Skidmore; our draftsmen don't work for free, in fact, we pay very well. But our net—. Are you familiar with the economics of design firms?"

"My husband is a consulting engineer," I answered.

"Individual practice doesn't count. The average large design firm spends about one-third of the gross fee on professional salaries, one-third on design costs and expenses, and the rest on overhead and profit. Net profit before taxes is about ten percent of the gross fees. Although they made a good living, few practicing architects get rich from their work."

"Don't I know it," I said, glancing at Pearl. "Lawyers can get rich, engineers can't."

"Well, that's almost true," he said. "The five of us, the four design partners and myself, are rich. I was quite well off before, and Bishop inherited a lot of money, but the other three didn't have a pot. Thanks to Roger, we're all millionaires."

"How did that happen?" Maybe I could learn.

"The average firm spends from five to fifteen percent of the gross on missionary work: getting business, publicity, presentations, preliminary designs, owner approval, things like that. Sometimes, with a committee, you make ten, fifteen, twenty analyses and preliminary designs before they even finalize their program. And then the project may be shelved or canceled or given to someone else."

"I know. My husband used to complain about idiot clients," I recalled bitterly.

"We never had that problem. Tom Bauer had a very simple approach. Give us the budget, the location, and your needs. Sign the contract, give us a big retainer, and that's it. The client had no right to make changes—midplan changes cost like the very devil—or even decisions. After all, Roger was a true genius, the greatest architect of all time. No patron could change the design of the ceiling of the Sistine Chapel, and no client could change a Talbott design."

"Why did they stand for it?" I asked.

"They loved it. These big executives hate to make decisions; every time they stick their necks out they can be wrong. Fortune 500 executives can't be wrong. In picking us they play safe. If someone complains that the design is lousy or that construction is over budget, the genius executive says that the best costs and the design is great, ask any critic. No one would dare criticize a Talbott design; it would brand you a Philistine. By selecting us you are safe from criticism and get lots of publicity as a patron of the arts."

"How does that translate into big profits?" asked Pearl.

"Let's talk numbers," R.C. replied. "Say the average fee for a major project is eight percent of gross construction cost. We charge one and one-half points more, because we're Talbott. The increase in the gross project cost to the client is negligible, especially since the government pays seventy percent of the cost. The rest can be charged off to public relations. That point and a half is all net to us."

Pearl looked puzzled. "How does an extra one and one-half percent make such a difference?"

"I told you before," R.C. was impatient. How could anyone not understand simple arithmetic? I guess he was learning that looks ain't everything. "If the normal profit is ten percent of eight percent, the net is point eight percent. If we get an extra one-point-five, we triple our net with no extra effort."

"That's wonderful," Pearl cooed. R.C. expanded. How quickly they forget.

"That isn't all. We don't make presentation drawings or revisions. Bauer just gives Roger the data. A couple of minutes and Roger hands the sketch to Erik. Erik and his group flesh it out in a couple of weeks and turn it over to Bishop. In two weeks we're in production. Four weeks later, Frank is working with the engineers and other specialists. We can turn out a job twenty percent faster than anyone else because of Roger. That adds another fraction of a point. By the time we're done, our profit is about three percent of job gross."

"How much did you do last year?" I asked, before Pearl could overdo the oohing and aahing.

"Almost two-hundred million." R.C. looked proud. "And we've got more than that on the books right now."

"R.C., you're talking about six million per year!" For

that kind of money I could get everybody in Bloomingdale's wiped out. In Zabar's, too. "That's the motive. One of you guys had to have done it."

He looked at me pityingly. "Mrs. Gold, you've got it exactly backwards. We've making this kind of money because of Roger. No Roger, no money. Of all the people who didn't want to see Roger dead, my partners and I head the list."

"Does that mean you'll go out of business, now?"

"Of course not, we're still a good firm; the other men are all tops in their field. It simply means we'll have to work a little harder and we'll get less for it. We've all discussed it and we're all agreed."

"Still, somebody wanted to kill him. And did."

"Not necessarily. Maybe young Candell didn't intend to kill Roger, but in the heat of the argument, lost his head and stabbed him."

"Aha! Argument! What argument? What did Roger want to see Jonathan about?" This is what I had been waiting for.

"It was a competition," R.C. explained, "for a large Senior Citizens' complex in the Sun Belt. A thirty-million-dollar budget."

"I thought your clients came to you on their hands and knees with their tongues hanging out," I said. "Why would you enter a design competition?"

"We shouldn't. Not only is it poor business, it is dangerous." R.C. shook his head at the stupidity.

"You could lose, right? Or, at least, not win."

"Same thing. When you're the greatest, you don't enter contests, you make clients come to you."

"So why did you do it?"

"Wanda, that's my wife, wanted us to. She's very interested in Senior Citizens. Actually, we're Seniors ourselves, legally. She wanted the best architect to do the best job so the poor people would have the most and the best. Also, she mentioned it to me privately and I never discussed it with the others; she was going to ask us to contribute our fee for a project to study aging. I think we would have done it; considering our tax bracket, I know I would have. Anyway, she's never asked a favor before, and we couldn't say no. Tom and Irma and I convinced Roger to enter; he's the majority stockholder and we needed his approval as well as the basic design."

"Even so, was it worth taking the chance?"

"Well, we were pretty sure of ourselves. This was an open competition, not one where there are, say, three preselected major architects. That meant that no other really top firms would compete; we would be the only ones with any prestige. Then, Roger was the best of all time; no judge would pass over him lightly. Last, one of the judges is the dean of the local school of architecture. He worships Roger's designs; his whole curriculum is practically a study of Roger's work. With him there, all we needed was one more vote out of the other two, although they usually make it unanimous for appearance's sake. And three years ago, Erik was on a design jury that picked the dean's firm's entry as a winner. One hand washes the other."

"Isn't that immoral?" Pearl, the innocent.

"Not at all. Just mutual respect and admiration."

"So you had it all locked up," I said.

"So we thought," said R.C. "Until Candell interfered. One month before he came to work for us, he'd submitted an entry to the same competition."

"So? Didn't you have it locked up?"

"Practically. Not one-hundred percent. Only trouble was, the other two judges liked his design very much. Even our friend, the dean, liked it."

"You're sure?" I asked. R.C. just looked at me. "Oh, I see. Deanie called you to tell you how funny it would look if the other two voted for Candell and he voted for Roger. Well, you can't win them all."

"Can't win them all?" R.C. choked. "Don't you see? The greatest architect of all time losing to a kid who isn't even a registered architect, and who works for Roger as a draftsman?"

"Yeah, humiliating."

"And expensive. Do you know what this could have cost us? We'd be laughed out of the business."

"I can see that. Once the bubble bursts—"

"Exactly. So the only business-like solution was for Candell to withdraw his entry." R.C. looked stern.

"You asked him to?" I wanted to keep him talking.

"Politely. I pointed out that it was unethical and unprofessional, now that he was an employee, to compete with his employer. I also told him that he had a great future with us if he did the right thing, and since he didn't have a chance of winning anyway—" R.C. looked at me shrewdly.

"He told you to shove it, right?"

"No. He agreed that his position wasn't moral, so he offered to resign."

"You refused?"

"Of course. Think how that would have looked. The only thing worse would have been to fire him. So I asked Tom to talk to him."

"No go?"

"Tom offered him a raise, like a fool. The kid took it to

be a bribe and got insulted. So I figured if Roger spoke to him. . . . He admired Roger's work."

"That's what the meeting was about?"

"Yes. Roger must have said the wrong thing to him, Candell lost his temper and killed Roger."

"Maybe Roger attacked him and it was self-defense."

He looked disgusted. "You think Roger brought a knife to the meeting? To kill Candell if he didn't agree to withdraw his design?"

"You don't think Jonathan brought the knife with him just in case he decided to get mad, do you? All he had to do was not go, right?"

"Well, someone brought that knife in and killed Roger with it. It could only have been Candell. Think about it."

I thought. Not good for the home team. "One more thing, R.C. Where were you at the time of the murder?"

"Right here, at home."

"Your wife will vouch for that?"

"My wife was out doing work on some charity, as usual."

"So you have no alibi."

"Neither do you, if I may be so rude."

"I didn't have any reason to kill Roger Talbott."

"Keep talking, Mrs. Gold," he answered, "you're doing just fine."

I decided I wasn't. We had just uncovered another motive which poor, moronic, panicky Jonathan had kept from his lawyer. If we told Burton about this, Alexander would have a new case to solve, a real easy one: The Brutal Dismemberment of the Rotten Client by a Formerly Rational Attorney. But if we didn't tell Burton now, if this additional motive came out during the trial, as it must, and caught Burton unprepared, Burton who prided himself on his careful preparation—Well, after Burton cooled down and did the only sensible thing, Pearl could live with us during the predivorce proceedings.

I was about to offer this to Pearl, provided, of course, that she did windows, when I saw she had that desperate crushed-flower look on her face I have seen too often on the face of a friend, so I did not say anything funny. I just put my arms around her tightly and lovingly, and assured her that it would not be necessary to mention this latest Jonathan stupidity to Burton because Alexander would find the real killer long before the trial.

I wish I believed that.

Even Bloomingdale's didn't help.

In the olden days, a king would kill the messenger who brought bad news. Today, on West 74th St., my lord and master tried to kill himself when I gave him the transcript of the taped R.C. Miller interview. He's not supposed to lose his temper; it could bring on a cardiac spasm.

I had made him a little card to carry around at all times. He had to read it whenever he felt himself getting angry. It said "Any fool who can make me angry can kill me." Even the act of taking it out of his pocket, the pause, was to give him time to realize the danger and to short circuit the process. If that didn't work, he had to turn it over and read the other side. That said "I'm the only fool who can make me angry." The only trouble was, reading it made him more angry. At me. For making him read the card. Naturally.

Everything was my fault. He explained it to me. Carefully. He had sent me out to find the killer, or at a minimum, to get enough information from R.C. to confirm Jonathan's innocence. Was that too much to ask, seeing that he had already proved Jonathan innocent and that all that was needed was a little more evidence for the D.A.?

"I sent you out to settle a few details, that's all. And what did you do?"

"What did I do?"

"You bring back another motive for conflict between Jonathan and Talbott. First, Jonathan knows about Talbott's trying to seduce his fiancée. Now Talbott is threatening him with God-knows-what professionally. The only thing the kid had going for him, other than my analysis, was no motive. Now I have two motives. Thank you very much."

"I know, darling, and I'm sorry. But I'll make up for my stupidity; I'll convince Pearl to confess she did it." I knew I shouldn't have said that, only I knew it after I said it. Fastest lip on the West Side.

There are times when Alexander has no sense of humor. "That's it!" he yelled. "You're off the case. I'll handle everything myself."

"But darling, you're not allowed to cross the street by yourself yet."

"Bring them here to my office."

"Sure. Who?"

"The other suspects, stupid."

"What other suspects? I didn't know we had even one suspect."

"The other architects. Talbott's partners. Isn't it clear that one of his partners did it?"

"No, it's not clear. They'd all lose from Talbott's death. Why should one of them want to kill him?"

"I don't care why," he answered impatiently. This from the same brain that had deduced that Jonathan was innocent because he had no motive. "I know one of them did it. It's obvious."

"It's obvious?" I couldn't help the idiot echo.

"Certainly." He was impatient with my blindness. Just as impatient as when he raked me over the coals because I left Jonathan's motive—two motives—out of my report. "It's clear that the key to the murder is getting in and out of Talbott's studio. An architect would be able to figure that out better than a layman. Also, it had to be someone who knew Talbott's habits and that Jonathan would be there at that time. Further, it had to be a business associate, since Talbott had no friends."

"Only friends kill people?" I asked. "How about enemies?"

"Norma," he was irritable, "stop arguing with me. Just get the suspects here, one at a time, in order of seniority. First one, tomorrow morning. Next one in the afternoon. Same thing the day after."

"*Zum befehl,* Herr Oberst. What inducement do I use? My fair white body?"

"Do I have to do everything for you? Think of a way."

"If I arrange it, will you promise not to get upset?"

"I promise," he yelled. "And I want reports on each one beforehand. Accurate ones," added nastily.

When you can't do something yourself, get someone else to do it for you. That's a Mrs. Gold's Law. A good executive becomes a great executive when he learns that; a woman knows it from birth. After all, what else are the filthy little beasts good for?

R.C., as senior partner, was the obvious choice to get the other four to talk to Alexander. The question was, could I act weak and helpless enough to appeal to his chivalry? Not bloody likely, since I'm twice his size and not the weepy type. Nor does coyness become me. My fair white body? For some stupid reason, most men are afraid of me, and besides, Alexander would kill R.C. if he found out. Assuming R.C. survived my ministrations.

So Pearl would have to volunteer. She volunteered. Did a terrific job; I didn't ask how. One of these days I'll have to check out comp lit.

XI

Thomas Bauer was a big, fat, tired looking man with heavy gray hair combed straight back. Alexander started right in. "Where were you at the time of the murder?"

"Now wait a minute," Bauer protested, "R.C. told us you wanted information, that's all."

"That's information."

"If you think I did it, you're barking up the wrong tree. Why should I kill the goose that laid the golden eggs?"

"I don't know why. Just tell me where you were."

"I was in my office, working."

"Any witnesses?"

"No, it was Sunday."

"Do you have to sign in at the lobby?"

"Yes, and out too, but that doesn't mean anything. Any architect knows there are doors in every office building that can easily be opened from the wrong direction if you know how."

"So you can't prove that you didn't sneak out, kill Talbott, and sneak in again."

"I don't have to prove it. The police already know who did it."

"Do you think Candell did it?" asked Alexander.

"It sure looks that way," Bauer answered.

"Why should he?"

"Maybe they quarreled. Roger was not the easiest person to get along with; he could be very abrupt with the lesser mortals."

"You included?"

"Everybody." Bauer shifted uneasily in his seat.

"Mr. Bauer, do you know Nina Slotkin?"

"I don't think so. Why?"

"Who does the hiring at Talbott Associates?"

"I do. I'm in charge of administration."

"Did Nina Slotkin apply for a summer job as a draftsman?"

Bauer hesitated. "We get hundreds of applications every year and I interview about forty people."

"I take it, you didn't hire her. Why not?"

"Probably there were others better qualified."

"Aren't you interested in hiring women?"

"Of course. With the Equal Employment Opportunity requirements, we bend over backwards to hire women and minorities."

"Yet you didn't hire Nina Slotkin."

"We hired two women and two minorities to fill nine summer positions. That's almost fifty percent."

"Tell me, Mr. Bauer," Alexander smiled the way he does when he announces mate in three, "tell me, how many short, plump, young blondes are employed by Talbott Associates?"

Bauer stared at Alexander for a full minute. "So you know," he said heavily.

"Yes," said Alexander, "let's talk about it."

"I turn them down for their own good. It's difficult for a young girl to be put under such pressure. Here's her boss, the greatest architect who ever lived, the man who can make or break her career, wanting her. If she refuses, she may find herself fired, maybe blackballed, her career ruined. She's too inexperienced to be sure. The trade doesn't work that way, and Roger would never hurt her; he's persistent but not vindictive, but she doesn't know that. If she accepts, she spends one afternoon with him and that's all. He never sees her again, talks to her, or even acknowledges her presence. It's as if he's looking for something he can never find. But she thinks it's her fault, some failing she has, that something is wrong with her. If it's the first time for her, she can be hurt very badly, psychologically. Either way, it's harmful to her. I avoid the problem by making sure that no one who looks like that ever works for us."

"There are hundreds like that out there in the wide, wide world."

"I can't help that. Whatever Roger does—did outside the office was his own business."

"Also, the firm can't be sued for sexual harassment."

"That, too," Bauer conceded.

"How long has Talbott been this way?"

"Ever since we moved to New York. Understand, he didn't want to hurt anyone, he just couldn't rest until he had the girl. Once. That was all. Like a sickness."

"Did his wife know?"

"Irma? I'm sure she didn't. It never spilled over into any part of his life or work. It was fully compartmentalized."

"Was Mrs. Talbott fooling around, too?"

"I wouldn't know. If she was, she was very discreet about it. There were always rumors, of course, but nothing definite."

"What kind of rumors?"

"Just catty stuff and innuendo. She was a very attractive woman who hung around with the artistic jet set, so some people—some women—might think she was like her friends. But I really doubt it."

"When you and she were working on the design of her house, did she ever make a pass at you?"

"Certainly not." Bauer looked uneasy. "People who didn't know her—she was a very social person, outgoing and friendly, almost the stereotype of the flirtatious Southern belle, but that was all there was to it, I'm sure. Inside she was completely different; very serious, always studying, working for charities, helping people."

"How did you find working with her?"

"Better than most clients. Don't forget, hanging around the office, she picked up quite a bit of architectural knowledge."

"What security precautions did you design into the house, Mr. Bauer?"

"There are wrought iron bars outside the windows of the lower three floors, and lockable safety gratings inside the windows of the upper two floors. Each entry has two locks, deadbolts, plus heavy sliding bolts, on both the outside and the vestibule doors, and the ground-floor front entrance has the iron grille door, locked, before you can even get to the outside door. That's because the ground-floor door is hidden from the street by the enclosure supporting the stair above, and a thief would have time to work on the outside door in privacy. There is no lock that can't be picked, you know, given enough time."

"Tell me about the alarm system."

"If any door or window is opened, even one inch, an alarm would ring at a central location. You turned it on when you left the house, and you had one minute to turn it off by a special key when you came home."

"Does that apply to the skylight and the roof scuttle too?"

"The scuttle, yes. The skylight is fixed in place, cannot be opened from the outside. Besides, how would anyone get on the roof? That block is solid houses on all four sides."

"From another house? Over the rooftops?"

"That's silly, Mr. Gold. If you know how to break into a house, why break into another house first, cross over the rooftops, and then break into the Talbott house? Why not break in directly?"

"What about entry through the back garden?"

"Same story. To get there you'd have to break into another house first. Why go to all the extra trouble?"

"What about Talbott's security system for his studio?"

"You mean the stairway doors? He didn't consult me on

that, but I understand it's very tight. That circuit even had a battery pack in the meter room which would keep it functioning for twenty-four hours if the Con Ed power failed."

"Why did he have the stairway there at all if he was so concerned about the privacy of his studio?"

"Emergencies. There had to be a way for him to get down if the elevator broke down or if there was a fire. When he set off the alarms by opening the doors, he could just tell his wife not to worry when he got downstairs."

"A professional question, Mr. Bauer. Why are there so many lavatories and bathrooms in that house?"

"Irma intended to do a lot of entertaining, throw big parties. There are never enough toilet facilities in any house to take care of that. Irma was determined that her house would be favored for parties, and it worked. Even some behind-the-scenes diplomatic meetings were held there; the ground-floor library is very private. She met lots of important people through her parties."

"And four bathrooms on the second floor?"

"One for each guest bedroom is required. And Irma and Roger led very different lives, came home at different times, so it was necessary to have two separate bathrooms and dressing rooms so they would not disturb each other."

"The third floor is practically a miniature health club."

"Exactly. Irma is very conscious of her looks. She used to be a little plump, you know, but now she is as slim as a model. But she hates to be alone, so she invites her friends—dancers, actors, singers—to work out with her. She helped some well-known entertainers before they became famous, and some of them are still her friends."

Alexander dropped this line, although I had the feeling

that at one time, at least, Bauer had been more than a little attracted to his partner's wife. "What is the firm working on now?" Alexander asked.

"We just got started on the General Conglomerates job, the last sketch Roger drew. Plus a good deal of work in progress. I'm spending a lot of time on the reorganization with R.C."

"What are your plans?"

"We're going to continue exactly as before; keep the same name and do the same work."

"What about Roger's stock?"

"We carry keyman insurance, a million on each of us and two on Roger, and the same to buy out the equity from heirs. R.C. arranged it. Otherwise we could end up with a wife as a partner." Bauer scowled at the thought.

"How could you continue to do the same work without Talbott?"

Bauer looked at Alexander as though wondering if he could trust him. Suddenly he blurted out, bitterly, "Roger was not an architect."

"Then how could he head a professional corporation?"

"He didn't. I did. The company has his name and he is the major stockholder, that's all. Back in Missouri, R.C. arranged it and, because Roger was so famous, no one made any difficulties. Here, I am president of the corporation and my license covers. My seal is on all plans and I am legally responsible. Two years ago Roger was licensed in New York State."

"So he finally passed the tests?"

"Certainly not. If he ever had taken the tests he wouldn't have scored one point out of one hundred. He never went to architectural school, never worked for an architect. He didn't even graduate from college."

"Then how did he get his license?"

"R.C. arranged it. The governor issued Roger an honorary license with full rights and privileges. After all, how would it look for the worlds greatest architect not to have a license to practice in his home state? We always make heavy contributions to campaign funds. That year they were heavier than usual."

"You sound a little bitter."

"A little. The famous Pyramid House, the one that started everything, who do you think designed it? Roger? All he did was sketch a pyramid with windows. I designed that house, and did pretty good job of it, considering what I had to work with. And Wilma, she was the one who wrote it up. Without us, Roger would still be working the carnivals."

"It sounds unfair," Alexander murmured provocatively.

"Damned right, it is. I was the architect of all the buildings that made us famous. Until we moved to New York, I did all the work; design, administration, coordination, client relations, everything. And for what? A lousy five percent."

"Didn't R.C. improve the position of all the partners?"

"Sure, but money isn't everything. I'm an architect; I design, create. Or at least I can. But I'm bogged down in administration. I haven't designed anything since I did my own home, eight years ago. Outside of a few people in the field, no one knows my name or respects my talents. Or recognizes that I am the architect who did all the early work."

"I'm in the field," said Alexander, "and I never heard of you."

"That's what I mean. The firm should have been Talbott and Bauer, at least. Or now, Talbott, Bauer, Bishop,

Dakin, and Kirsch. But even with him dead, it will still be Roger Allen Talbott Associates, P. C."

"Couldn't you have changed it?"

"Sure we could, but we all decided that we would be better off keeping the old name. No layman knows of any of us, not even Kirsch, who is in charge of design."

"So, Mr. Bauer," Alexander said, "you had a motive for killing Roger Talbott."

Bauer looked shocked. "Is that what was on your mind?"

"Well, the jealousy, the anger, the feeling of being cheated. . . . People have killed for less."

"Then you don't understand what I've been telling you. I, we, any of us, could have left the firm, dissolved the firm, anytime we wanted. Why didn't we? None of us liked him, not even his father-in-law. We stuck with him because his name brought in the business. You think a firm called Bauer, Bishop, Dakin, and Kirsch would be given a job like the General Conglomerates Tower? It would go to Skidmore or Pei or Johnson. Roger was the front for the firm. A damned good firm, if I say so myself, run by a bunch of real pros with talent and skill. None of us would be doing anything more than tract houses if it weren't for the Talbott name. So why should I kill him?"

"It seems to me that none of you will suffer financially by his death."

"How do you figure that?" asked Bauer.

"If the insurance buys out Mrs. Talbott's equity, each of you gets twice the percentage of profit."

"You're assuming the volume remains constant without Talbott. It won't. R.C. projected a fifty-percent decrease for the next three years."

"So at least you're no worse off than before."

"Wrong again. We can't shove a pyramid down a client's throat anymore. We'll have to go the normal route: presentations, revisions, the works, and frankly, I prefer it that way. We'll be in the same position as other architects and our take-home money will be half of what it was before."

"Which is still a lot of money."

"I'm not crying, but what happened to the motive, Mr. Gold? Am I going to kill a man so I can have the pleasure of cutting my income in half?" Bauer's face was flushed.

"Ad you said, Mr. Bauer, money isn't everything. Maybe you hated him enough to kill him."

"Hate Roger? How do you hate a nothing?" Bauer got up angrily and stalked out, slamming the door.

"Gee, boss," I said as soon as the door closed, "that sure was a masterful interrogation. Now will you reveal the name of the dastardly killer so we can all go home?"

"Stop with the sarcasm, Norma," he growled.

"Sarcasm? Me? Didn't you detect the adulation in my voice? Now that I am off the case and no longer hindering you, I figured you would have it all wrapped up."

"I am trying to get all the information I can so that a pattern will emerge."

"My reports aren't accurate?"

"It's not the same. When I'm face-to-face with them I can get nuances which may lead to new areas."

"So why do you need us here? Go be a big hero detective all by yourself."

"With Pearl here, there is less of a feel of interrogation; she softens the atmosphere. She can also watch the suspects closely as we talk, detect physical sets and expressions. She's very sensitive to these things." Meaning I'm not.

"So what am I here for?" After all these years I still haven't learned not to ask leading questions.

"Well, you know I am still physically weak. You're a big girl, no one would dare to attack me with you around." Norma Gold, hired gun to one of the strongest men in New York. Equal Employment Opportunity. Thrilling.

I sent Pearl out with Alexander for his walk. The tape from Bauer's interview went into Pearl's machine to be transcribed later. Then I made a list of jobs that would take her a year to finish. That would teach her to be so goddamned sensitive.

I put the Bishop report on Alexander's desk, a fresh tape in the recorder, and a brandy into me. I deserved it.

XII

Imagine Cary Grant six-feet-four-inches tall, with heavy auburn hair and light hazel eyes, shoulders almost as wide as Alexander's but with a waist a teenager would envy, dressed in navy slacks and a pale blue shirt with short sleeves that showed rippling muscles under a lightly tanned skin. Add a beautiful deep voice, Continental manners, perfect teeth and a confident smile. Let Pearl probe his psyche, I would just look.

Alexander, with his usual delicacy, said, "I understand you're a homosexual."

Bishop smiled sweetly and said, "When the urge strikes me. Tell me about your wife's sexual proclivities."

Alexander stiffened. "The point is not well taken. I am investigating a murder."

"And I," replied Bishop, "am investigating the investigator, whose prejudice may cause me and my company harm."

"Your sexual aberrations may have a bearing on the case."

"As much bearing as your wife's?"

"Can you assure me of that?"

"If you would take the word of a killer, yes."

Alexander, having no way to win this one, changed the subject. "You look like someone who works out with weights."

"I do. You look like someone who should work out more with weights. And eat less."

Alexander was starting to get that look in his eyes. Here was a stranger challenging him in his own home, a homosexual who was fast of tongue and large of muscle, who would put Alexander down in front of me and Pearl, and who would win because he was more waspish than Alexander could ever be. And Alexander was too weak to challenge him to any test of will, strength, or intelligence.

So I stepped in. "Do you also jog, Mr. Bishop?"

He looked shocked. "Certainly not. Jogging in the city is for fools. Aside from the inherent problems, that even if you're tired you still have to get back; that if you get a stroke or heart attack you are helpless and far from home; sudden rain, excessive heat . . . there are the specific city problems: muggers, crazies, dog dirt, cars, bicycles, people, everything. To breathe that poison: carbon monoxide, nitrogen oxides, sulphides, tars, to take that into your lungs and call it beneficial. . . ." He shook his head.

"Many people jog in the city," I said. "They look healthy and happy."

"On the outside," he answered. "Inside, they're a mess. Erik jogs every day. I've spoken to him about it but he doesn't listen. He's practically bald and looks much older than I do, though he's three years younger. In ten years he'll look like Tom Bauer. Tom's only twelve years older, but he looks like my grandfather."

"He does look older than his years."

"It's the junk he eats. And no exercise. I give him five more years, and bang, a heart attack."

"Yes, overweight will do that for you," I said, glancing at Alexander. Mistake. This brought him back into the conversation.

"Mr. Bishop," said Alexander, "You live in a huge loft building. Alone. Isn't it too big for you?"

"I've fixed it up exactly the way I like it."

"It must be interesting. May I see it?"

"Only my friends can come in."

"But," said Alexander, glancing at the report before him, "it is well known that you haven't any friends." Bishop smiled, as at a clever child.

Alexander took another tack. "What do you do at Talbott Associates?"

"I'm in charge of all the architects and draftsmen, except for Frank's people and Erik's design team. I make sure that the working drawings are produced on time, complete and accurate, properly detailed and referenced, and within the budget. Well within."

"You have the reputation for being one of the best at this," Alexander was being conciliatory.

"I am *the* best. Everyone knows that."

"Slave driver?" Alexander was being facetious.

"Certainly not." Bishop was insulted. "Overpushing will produce temporary gain, but the sag afterwards will more than wipe it out. I just apply intelligence."

"How?"

"Space, for example. You know the average drafting room, row on row of tables, no room between, squeezed in to get the maximum number of people working per square foot."

"You disagree with this?"

"Not if your goal is the most people per square foot. I want maximum production per dollar."

"Aren't the two the same?" I asked.

He looked at me, disgusted. "I give each of my people forty square feet more space. Then I put a partition around each one, giving him his own little room. With sound insulation, shelves for reference books, a cork-board. He has quiet, a personal atmosphere, no visual interruptions, no conversations with his neighbors."

"Doesn't this cost?"

"Sure. Twenty-five dollars a square foot rent times forty equals one thousand per year. If this increases production as little as ten percent . . . figure it out. Average salary, twenty-five thousand; billing three times that. Net is ten percent of billing, seventy-five hundred dollars per year. If I get another ten percent production, my net goes up seventy-five hundred dollars per man per year. All for one thousand dollars."

"Amazing," Pearl purred. Wasted. Not entirely; flattery is still appreciated, even from a woman.

"That's not all. Lighting. I put one-hundred-foot candles uniformly on the drafting table. Reduces fatigue and improves performance with no extra effort. I provide a full set of references, standards, and details in every room; no searching for information away from the desk. The best equipment, the finest drafting machine, a computer, dimension adder, electric eraser, electric lead sharpener, everything."

"Is that cost effective, duplicating all the references and equipment?"

"Payback is fourteen months. I also have central equipment, computerized files, computer drafting, the latest."

"Don't they go crazy, cooped up in a little cubicle?"

"They can leave any time they want to, no one stands over them with a whip. I have a room with recliners they can use anytime, bars to hang from, best thing for draftsman's back."

"What about coffee breaks?"

"All day long is breaktime. I have a girl with a cart going around from room to room. But no caffeine; fruit juices, skim milk, sugarless granola bars, vegetable juices, raw vegetables, and fresh fruit organically grown. No charge."

"You mean they don't pay for it?"

"Not directly. Nothing is really free, of course, but any employee can take whatever he wants whenever he wants. We take it off our taxes as an expense; they don't have to pay for it with aftertax dollars. Everyone benefits. Especially since it isn't necessary to leave your desk. Also free vitamin and mineral supplements. Yoghurt, kefir, wheat germ, brewer's yeast, we have it all."

"Can you afford this?"

"We profit. The trade average is about eight days of sick leave per year; our average is less than one. A healthy employee is a happy employee."

"What do you do about smoking?"

"No smoking allowed. I won't have my kids poisoned.

Do you know how much time smoking wastes? Not just in sickness, I mean production. Have you ever watched a pipe smoker?"

"Has anyone ever tried to sneak a cigarette? After all, he's in his own cubicle."

"Once in a while a new man tries. He only tries it once. I spray his cubicle, his cigarettes, and him, from top to bottom, with Lysol."

"Spray him?" Alexander was astounded. "Did anyone ever take a poke at you?"

"You're pretty big," answered Bishop. "Would you like to take a poke at me?"

I got ready to jump in between. No one ever talks to Alexander that way. He thought for a moment, looked Bishop up and down, then said quietly, "No, I don't think so." Didn't even get red. Great work, darling. I'm proud of you. Finally you're learning to live with your condition.

Bishop nodded slightly at the implicit compliment.

"How do your employees feel about working this way?"

"They love it. It's not just the freebies and the good health. They take pride in their work and their productivity; the respect they earn for their accomplishments. We pay pretty well, too. Base pay is about seven percent above any other firm in the area, so we get the best. We have a good profit-sharing system and I give special bonuses for super productivity. Anyone who works for me, my way, can end up with twenty percent more than if he worked anywhere else."

"How did Roger like the way you did things? Did you and he ever differ about it?"

"Roger never set foot in my space; he wouldn't dare. He had no idea of what I did and, as far as I know, never gave a damn."

"The head architect of your company didn't know what you did?"

"I only saw him at annual meetings and I made a point not to talk to him. He was a creep and a bore. Not a professional, a goddamned dilettante."

"But you went to Europe with him to do two major projects."

"Erik and I went to Europe to do two major jobs; Roger was there for show. He sat in on one meeting in Salzburg and one in Munich. Didn't open his mouth, thank God. Made two sketches, that was the extent of his contribution. As far as I was concerned, he wasn't there."

"Where did he go?"

"No place. Just sat around in some square while Erik and I were working."

"Doing what?"

"Trying to finalize two major projects at the same time. Like all designers, Erik is normally a temperamental wreck, and I thought he was really going to go off the deep end this time. But after the first week, suddenly, for no apparent reason, he calmed down, relaxed, and really produced.

"He did all the design work?"

"Of course. That's what he was there for."

"Then what did you do there?"

"Acted wise, mature, and business-like. Don't forget, Erik is the designer, I'm production. I helped, but it was his ball game."

"Then why did you go at all?"

"Two of us were needed, one to stay on in each city to complete all the details. Also Erik is younger than I am; at that time he looked like a baby. He's a good architect, maybe even a great one, but no one was about to give two big jobs to a kid who looked as if he shaved once a week. Besides, he had no head for business. Good with the charcoal, but couldn't figure a ten-percent markup without a computer. Also, Tom and Frank were married, and I had the language."

"You speak German?"

"I speak five languages perfectly, four rather well, and another four adequately. I also read classical Greek, Latin, and Hebrew."

"So you and Mrs. Talbott were at loose ends?"

"I was not; she was. The second day there she even asked me to escort her to a concert. Very coy and girlish."

"Why you? Didn't she know?"

"I've never made a secret of it. But she was going stir crazy and Roger just didn't go anywhere, even with her. She isn't so stupid as to pick up strange men in a foreign country where the signals can be misinterpreted. Erik is definitely not a music lover. So she had to come to me first."

"I take it you refused her."

"Politely at first, then bluntly."

"Was she angry? Did she vow vengeance on you? Or on her husband for not taking her out?"

"Miffed slightly would describe it. She was used to Roger's not going out, and it would gain her nothing to feud with me. She had a very short attention span; just announced that I was no gentleman and flounced off, saying that she would make Erik take her."

"Did he?"

"I guess so. Erik was pretty junior in the firm, and she was the wife of the boss. And she was also young and attractive, if that type is to your taste."

"That being the case, why didn't you take her to the

concert yourself? Why make an enemy of Mrs. Talbott?"

"If a man is known by the enemies he keeps, having her for an enemy could only enhance my reputation. I am very particular about my social life. I have no objection to the company of women, but they must meet the same standards I set for my male acquaintances."

"Mrs. Talbott did not?"

"Mrs. Talbott is a conceited, stupid, bubbleheaded phony. And even if she were not, I would not associate with the wife of a creep."

"You seem to know her well."

"I spoke to her once. It was enough."

"So you hung around Europe alone?"

"Your smarmy voice tells me you are asking a different question. I did have some adventures there. Nothing permanent, it never is. But I did not hang around Austrian schoolyards seducing little blond boys. Or," he hesitated, "or little blonde girls."

"So you know," said Alexander.

"Everybody knows," replied Bishop.

"Mrs. Talbott, too?"

"I don't think she knows anything other than what her gurus at The New School tell her."

"Why do you have such a low opinion of her?"

"I gave you the adjectives before."

"What do you think of your partners?"

"Erik is very talented, erratic, nervous, one-sided, and unhealthy. Frank is competent, a religious nut, unhealthy, and dull, dull, dull. Tom is good with clients, pompous, stodgy, beer-pretzels-TV, and very, very unhealthy. R.C. is clever, good with numbers, a small-town sharpie who hasn't read a book in his life, and unhealthy."

"You left out Roger Talbott."

"A clod, a stone, a worse-than-senseless thing. If no one had told me he was dead, I wouldn't have known."

"You hated him?"

"I didn't know him well enough to hate him, but if I had, I am sure I would have."

"How do you like the design of his house?"

"Mr. Gold, subtlety is not your forte. I was never in the Talbott house, even when I didn't kill him. If I had been in it, I wouldn't have liked it. I don't associate with my partners. We have nothing in common but the company."

"You don't like them?"

"I thought I had made that clear."

"Do they like you?"

"Like has nothing to do with it. I am very good at my work. I produce."

"You have no need for money. Why do you work?"

"Like all reasoning humans, I must do what I can as well as I can do it."

"You could go elsewhere, work with people you like and respect."

"There are very few people I either like or respect; none that I both like and respect. I doubt if I could run my department my way anywhere else. I would have to be a partner in some large organization and have weak partners who would not interfere, who lacked my skills and talents but were competent in their own ways. If I found such a group, how would that be different from what I have now?"

"You're rich enough to form your own firm."

"What's the point in cheating at solitaire?"

"How will Roger's death affect you?"

"It may be an improvement. It was a real sweat to produce his shitty designs, even after Erik worked them out."

"Won't there be less business and lower profits?"

"In three years we'll be making more than ever."

"Where were you when Roger was killed?"

"In the Metropolitan Museum."

"Any special area?"

"I spent a little time with Schiele and Munch."

"And Ensor?"

Bishop lifted an eyebrow. "And Ensor."

"But not Bacon?" Alexander pressed.

"No."

"Not subtle enough?"

"Precisely."

"See anyone you know?"

"There are very few people I wish to know."

"So you have no alibi."

"No. Do you?"

"I am not a suspect."

"Neither am I. The murderer has been arrested."

"He didn't do it."

"Pity. I would have given him a medal. For leaving the world a little better than he found it."

"John Chapelle Bishop," Alexander spoke firmly, "did you kill Roger Allen Talbott?"

"No," Bishop smiled, "and I can prove it."

"How?"

"Alexander Magnus Gold, anyone who knows me, knows that I would never stab a creep in the back from behind. It's not my style."

"What is your style, Mr. Bishop?"

"I would stab a creep from in front." He stood up and

moved gracefully toward the door. "So I could watch his eyes as he died." He smiled angelically as he left.

As soon as Bishop was gone, Pearl shuddered. "He's scary."

"He's crazy," I said definitively.

"You're both right," Alexander agreed.

"Isn't there something that can be done about a person like that?" Pearl asked.

"What?" I replied. "Put him in jail? Commit him to a mental institution? Go prove something. If he killed Talbott, we'll never be able to catch him; he's too smart. He's functioning very well in his work. His social life is his own business. He's very rich and he looks normal. Better than normal; like Superman would like to look."

"He has surrounded himself," said Alexander, "with the people and the environment he can control; that's the basis of his being able to live. He's made a sealed box of his life; everything in that box works exactly the way he wants. Everything outside the box is kept outside, firmly."

"Wouldn't he kill someone who disturbed the way he lives? If Talbott did something to break that box, wouldn't Bishop kill him?" I looked at Alexander in fear. I did not want him to go up against Bishop, especially now, especially if Bishop were the killer.

"There is so much violence in that man, that if it ever escaped, Bishop could have killed Talbott," replied Alexander, "and his wife, and his in-laws, and the whole city in which they lived, no limit. Killing one man would mean nothing to him."

"What is a man like that doing living alone in a big loft?" asked Pearl. "I should think he'd have a small suite in a hotel near the office."

"That would be too confining in body and spirit," I told

her. "He has a powerful mind, in case you didn't notice." Pearl hadn't taken her eyes off Bishop's muscles for a second. Although he's attractive in a well-groomed Wall Street way, in bathing trunks, Burton looks like a fat white slug.

"He needs room as well as control," said Alexander. "He cannot stand being limited by others or living according to their rules. That building is not just a home, it's his world. In that world, no one challenges him, no one competes. He is God of all he surveys."

"He challenged you before," I pointed out. Someday I won't say the wrong thing to my husband.

Alexander flushed. "He must have known I was helpless. When I'm well maybe we'll see who is the better man." He must have seen me eyeing Bishop, too. Poor baby, I was just looking. Please realize, you'll never get better; the scar on your heart will never go away. You'll never be able to fight again, compete so aggressively again. The most I hope for is a quiet life, a shielded life, for you. Shielded by me. I'm willing.

I recovered quickly. "I think it was clever to act helpless so early. He opened up after he thought you were not up to him physically."

He looked at me mistrustfully, but said nothing.

"I'd like to see the inside of Bishop's house," Pearl said. "He's a real killer type and I'll bet we find lots of clues."

"That's a great idea," I enthused. "We'll sneak in Friday morning while he's at work."

"No!" Alexander slapped the table hard. "Positively not! Are you both crazy? At best, the two of you would end up in jail. More likely you would be dead. That house of his is a sealed fortress. He can't allow any intrusion. Don't you understand what you are dealing with? The worst thing that could happpen is that you might get in; you'd never get out."

"But if he's the killer, don't we need the evidence?" Pearl was torn.

"I don't know who the killer is yet," said Alexander.

"He's the killer," said Pearl. "I'm sure of it."

"Except for maybe Roger Talbott, I'm sure he's never killed anyone. In his eyes, he has already beaten everyone, so why should he bother."

"Just to prove he could do it," answered Pearl.

"If he is the strongest," said Alexander thoughtfully, "he need never be put to the test. He wins by overwhelming, intimidating, physically and psychologically. He doesn't compete, ever. He never has to fight."

"But he is fighting, Alex, every minute. He is so tense, always preparing for the battle. He is *so* competing, Alex, I can tell."

"In that sense, Pearl, you're right."

"But who is he competing with, Alex? Who is he fighting?"

"Death," he answered softly, "death."

XIII

The next morning, at precisely ten o'clock, Frank Dakin arrived, a slim, sandy-haired man of average height and appearance; his only unusual feature was his deep-set, burning blue eyes.

Alexander looked up from my report. "According to the record, you were born on the same day as Saint Francis Xavier, you were named after him, you were studying to become a Jesuit, and your grades were good. Why did you drop out?"

"I had a nervous breakdown."

"Suicidal?"

"Suicide is a mortal sin." Dakin tensed visibly.

"If not yourself, would you kill another?"

"I would not break the Commandments."

"If you were faced with a situation where you had to break one Commandment to preserve another, what would you do?"

"Mr. Gold, don't try to be a theologian; you haven't the skill for it, nor the background. God gave man free will within the limits of His Holy Laws. Man can choose between Good and Evil. Faced with such a choice, as all men are sooner or later, I would choose for the Good."

Alexander started to respond, but, sensibly changed the subject. "What made you decide to become an architect?"

"After I recovered, I had a dream three nights running. I was building a golden tower to Heaven so that those who loved God could ascend to the foot of The Throne to bask in the Holy Light." Dakin's eyes glowed.

"Have you achieved your goal?"

"In my own way, I am trying to fulfill my mission on Earth." His right eyelid began twitching.

"As I understand it, your function in the firm is to turn the architectural plans into a completed building." After Bishop, Alexander was trying to be cordial.

"Not quite that," Dakin said. "Tom gets the work, Erik does the design, John produces the working drawings, I coordinate them with the engineers, add the specs, supervise the construction, check shop drawings and samples, and approve requisitions. Then R.C. collects the money."

"You didn't mention Talbott. Wasn't he the most important part of the process?"

"He did the sketch for the client that Erik worked from." His right hand began trembling.

"Isn't the initial concept, the flash of creation, the most important part?"

"Mr. Gold," Dakin said, "you're an engineer, surely you know better. Anyone could have made that sketch, even Tom, who hasn't touched a pencil in years."

"You're telling me Talbott served no purpose in the firm?"

"Practically none, and he liked it that way."

"Talbott Associates will suffer no loss by his death?"

"We'll lose some business at first, but in the end, we'll all be better off, even financially."

"Money is important to you?"

"Very important. God has placed me in a position where I can build my golden tower, where I can support many worthy causes. The more I earn, the better I can help."

"So Roger's death was a godsend to you and the causes you support."

"In that sense, yes."

"You wouldn't have helped matters along a little, would you?"

"It was God's will that Talbott should die without my help." Dakin's eyelid was now twitching rapidly.

"Where were you when Talbott was killed?"

"St. Patrick's Cathedral."

"Isn't that close to the Talbott House?"

"Very. I got there at nine-thirty and left at ten-thirty."

"Perfect timing. Anyone see you entering or leaving?"

"None who remember me. The police checked."

"Why did you go to the Cathedral at that time?"

"I go to church often, not just for Mass. I go to pray, to meditate, to contemplate. To feel closer to God."

"Isn't God everywhere?"

"I do not go to church for God's benefit, but for my own. I can concentrate better in the quiet darkness; the outside world does not intrude. I can relax, be sheltered, calm, at peace."

"What troubles you?"

"Myself. My inadequacies and lapses, my inability to function as well as I wish in carrying out God's will on Earth. The presence of Evil in the universe."

"You work closely with John Bishop. Isn't he evil?"

"John? Of course not. Evil is deliberate, continuous, pervasive, working against God's way. John can't help himself; he is slave, not master. I pray for his soul. Not for him, for I do not believe he will change on Earth, but for his immortal soul."

"Would not the world be better off if John Bishop were removed from it?"

"That may be so from your point of view, or even mine. It may also be, that in the eye of God, John does more good than evil, on balance. Do not the mosquito and the disease microbe flourish? If John were truly evil, God would have removed him."

"Through human agency?"

"That is one way."

"The way Talbott was removed?"

"Or by lightning bolt, snakebite, earthquake, whatever is at hand." Dakin put his trembling hand in his pocket.

"Bishop is a sinner, is he not?"

"There is yet time for him to prepare himself to be in a state of grace when he meets his Maker."

"Talbott was a sinner, too, wasn't he?"

"We are all sinners. Flesh is weak."

"But I'm talking about Talbott in particular." Alexander's voice grew hard. "Tell me, Frances Xavier Dakin, tell me, is your wife short, blond, and blue-eyed?" Dakin jumped up, glaring. Alexander continued, "Are your daughters short, blond, and blue-eyed?"

Dakin spoke in a tightly controlled voice through clenched teeth, his eyes blazing. "Mr. Gold, my children, daughters and sons, were brought up in the love of God and in a good moral atmosphere. That does not change, ever, in a lifetime. Roger's perversions never touched my family. Although I know you said this to provoke, rather than out of conviction, I find it insulting. Goodbye."

"You sure hit a nerve that time," I said after Dakin had left.

"I think it's pretty clear," said Pearl, "that Talbott and one of Dakin's daughters—"

"No," Alexander broke in. "If that had happened, and Dakin found out, he would have killed Talbott right then and there. And he would have felt he was an instrument of God removing Evil."

"What do you think the connection is?" Pearl asked.

"I think Talbott propositioned the oldest Dakin daughter when she was very young, fifteen or so. She didn't know how to handle it, so she told her mother, which speaks well for the strength of that family and Mrs. Dakin in particular. Mrs. Dakin went to Talbott and told him quietly that if he ever went near any of her children again, she would have her brothers break his legs."

"Why didn't Dakin do something?"

"His wife never told him," I explained. "Knowing how near the edge he is at all times—you see how tightly tense he is—she was afraid it would trigger a murder. So, like a good wife, she handled the problem herself, without troubling her husband."

"But Dakin knows something," said Pearl. "I can tell."

"Of course," Alexander responded. "He isn't a fool. He probably noticed little anomalies. Maybe his wife saw to it that her children never accepted invitations to Talbott parties. Or that Talbott avoided him more than usual, or never spoke to Mrs. Dakin. Whatever it was, he is almost certain that something happened."

"But he's holding it in," I added. "He can't admit it."

"And his daughters are at the age where they are almost women," Pearl said. "That is a difficult time for any man; for one like Dakin, it must be hell."

"Yes," I said, "and did you notice he said that Alexander insulted him—not offended, insulted—when he only asked if Dakin's wife and daughters were short, blond, and blue-eyed. Even if Alexander had asked if Talbott lusted for his daughters, why should Dakin be insulted? Unless he takes his daughters' sexual attractiveness as a promise of sin."

"He does. He sees the world as evil," said Alexander. "Not only original sin, but an active trending toward evil. And he feels that he should do more to help good triumph."

"What made you ask about Dakin's daughters in the first place?" Pearl asked.

"It was obvious," he said.

"Obvious again, Alexander?" I asked. "Forty pages of Talmudic-logic-obvious or something we poor mortals can handle?"

"Simple *and* obvious," he answered. "Just from asking the right questions. Here's a seminarian, preparing for at least thirteen years of study to become a Jesuit, dedicated, obedient, and celibate. A young man, his blood eighty-proof testosterone. Suddenly he drops out, nervous breakdown. Why? He was caught robbing the poorbox? He changed his dedicated mind? He wanted to become a Moonie? Sex, that's what. The drive was too much for him; he couldn't handle it, so he had a nervous breakdown. And he's still ready to explode about sex; you saw him."

"Granted," said Pearl. "But how does that tell you that his oldest daughter is blond, blue-eyed, and short?"

"Stab in the dark," he admitted, "but not a guess. If Talbott had anything to do with a girl, she had to look like his mother when he was a baby. Norma's report on Dakin left out a few little details, such as the sex and age of his children, the color of their eyes and hair, what his wife looked like, everything that was important. I had to figure out that, as an devout Catholic, Dakin was probably married and had a large family; that if he was short and blue-eyed, and sort of blond, his daughters were the same. When he jumped up when I asked him about his wife, I knew I was right."

"I'm sorry I left out the filling in his wife's left bicuspid," I said, "but I have to decide what's relevant and what isn't. I can't put everything into a report."

"For me you can," he answered, "and you'd better. I'm the one who decides what's important and what isn't."

"Yes, master," I said soothingly. He had done it again: *Overkill* by Alexander Magnus Gold. Next report I made on a suspect, I would put in what he ordered: everything. The first seventeen hundred pages would take us to the suspect's first birthday, then the report would start to really grow long. And Alexander would have to keep his big mouth shut until, frustrated up to here, he would have to admit that all the data is as useless as no information.

"You know," said Pearl suddenly, "they're all crazy, the whole bunch of them. Architects—you never think of certain types, dentists, accountants, architects, as being unstable—but these guys, one is nuttier than the other. I'll bet that Kirsch is just as loony as the rest of them."

"Well, Pearl," Alexander pontificated, "everyone has his little quirks. It all depends on the point of view. Why, I'm sure that there are some people who would find even me a little odd." He smiled at the very idea.

So did I.

XIV

Erik Kirsch came promptly at 3:30, brilliant in purple and gold jogging shorts, shirt, and headband. A tall, slim, handsome man with thinning blond hair flecked with gray, he had the tense, skittish look of a racehorse.

As soon as he sat down, Alexander started. "Well, Mr. Kirsch, I guess the burden is on your shoulders now."

"What burden?" Kirsch asked.

"Why, doing all the basic design for Talbott Associates."

"I've been doing that ever since I started with the company." Kirsch looked miffed.

"Not that, Mr. Kirsch. I mean what Roger used to do. The original concept, the genius part."

Kirsch flushed. "Mr. Gold, Roger never designed anything in his life; not buildings, not doghouses, nothing. He just made little sketches, ten-second line drawings, boxes with pyramids on top."

"Doesn't his genius lie in that simplicity? After all, his buildings have won dozens of awards."

"Not his buildings, my buildings. You think Talbott

knew anything about architecture? He didn't know a cricket from a wicket; he couldn't even read a plan. For all he knew, our buildings could have been filled with concrete."

"That's not the way I heard it," retorted Alexander. "What about the latest Talbott design, the General Conglomerates Building?"

"The famous cathedral to free enterprise?" Kirsch sneered. "You know what I got from our genius? In cross section, four squares coming off a central square, like a Red Cross symbol. Five rectangular prisms stood on end, each topped with a pyramid. Proportioned for twenty stories. The simp didn't even know how big the building was to be."

"That's incredible," said Alexander, incredibly.

"It's true. I lengthened the four outer towers to fifty-three stories, and the core tower to sixty. I elongated the top pyramids to spires, the four slimmer outer spires balancing the higher, bigger, middle spire. I moved the outer towers away from the central core, bridging at the elevator transfer floors to create flying buttresses all around and stiffening the complex against wind load. Then I turned the plan forty-five degrees on the plot to make eight triangular plazas at the base. *I* designed that building, not Roger Talbott. If he had lived to see it built, he wouldn't have recognized it."

"All right, all right," said Alexander, trying to calm him down. "All I knew was what I read in the papers."

"The papers? What do they know? Ask anyone in the business. Anyone." Kirsch was still glowering.

"Well, even so," said Alexander, "didn't using his sketches save money? No presentations, no redesigns?"

"I'll bet R.C. told you that. You know how much time my people spend trying to make architecture out of those damned little sketches? How much time Tom puts in convincing clients that those stupid pyramids are good? How much it costs John in extra drafting, computing, dimensioning, detailing? Extra plans, sections, and elevations? Frank kills himself to make the engineering fit. You think this doesn't cost? And what about potential clients who hear stories about going over budget? I don't mean five percent, I'm talking about fifty. You think that brings repeat business? We've never done a second job for a business client. I don't mean government agencies, they're spending your money so what the hell, I mean real clients. So tell me, Mr. Gold, how do we save money?" Kirsch looked at Alexander challengingly.

"Aren't you guys supposed to be the richest architects in New York?"

"We earned it the hard way, and we'll do a lot better without him."

"I take it you didn't like Talbott?"

"Nobody liked Talbott; not me, not any of us, not his wife, not his maid, and if he had a dog, the dog wouldn't have liked him either. What was there to like? He was nothing."

"Is that a reason for you to kill a man? Because he was a nothing, and not liked?"

"Is that what you were leading up to? I thought you wanted facts. So excuse me, I was just kidding. We all loved Roger Talbott, good old lovable Roger."

"You certainly sounded as though you hated him enough to kill him."

"Not hated, Mr. Gold, despised. If I had killed him, would I have told you how I felt?"

"Maybe. You could be trying reverse psychology."

"Yes, but Professor Moriarty, you know that I know

that you really know that I really know. . . ." Kirsch let his voice fade away.

Alexander had to smile. "All right. Let's talk about something else. Where were you when Talbott was killed."

"Jogging. In Central Park."

"Witnesses?"

"Hundreds."

"Anyone you know?"

"Well, if you run the same course at the same time every day, you tend to see familiar faces. And backs."

"Did you?"

"I think so. But except for one, none that I can really remember. I jog seriously, concentrate on my inner self."

"Which one do you remember?"

"A girl. I used to see her running in the opposite direction weekends. A very beautiful girl, tall, with black hair down to her waist. Striking figure, like a showgirl's. That day she was wearing only a tiny pair of shorts and a thin cotton undershirt. She was soaking wet, with no bra. Beautiful. I'm sure she smiled at me."

"So you have an alibi."

"Not exactly. We crossed near the Museum sometime before ten. I'm sure the police spoke to her, but no one told me anything. The trouble is, they didn't find anyone who remembered me at the south end of the park, or the west side, after ten."

"Have you spoken to that girl since?"

"I don't even know her name. She hasn't been jogging there since." Kirsch looked a little wistful.

"Erik, if any of your associates killed Talbott, which one would it be?"

"None of them. It would have been easier to walk away and form a new corporation."

"Why didn't you?"

"Inertia, I guess. We had discussed it before, but we weren't ready yet."

"You all discussed it as a group?"

"Not formally, just at lunch."

"With R.C. too?"

"Not directly. After all, he was Roger's father-in-law. But he knew we were unhappy. He's too good a businessman to let family interfere with business."

"Could you legally have left Talbott Associates and formed a new firm?"

"It would have been tricky. We might have had to walk away and leave the whole company to Roger. Might even have had to relocate to another part of the country."

"Give away a multimillion-dollar business?"

"It wouldn't be a ten-dollar business without us."

"Couldn't Roger have gotten new associates?"

"Roger couldn't organize a peanut stand. R.C. would have been able to do it, though."

"So it all depended on R.C.'s joining with the rest of you."

"That would have been an important consideration."

"Had any of you approached R.C. on this?"

"How could we unless we knew in advance that he would be with us?" He seemed irritated at Alexander's obtuseness.

"A real Catch-22 situation, which could easily be resolved by removing Roger Talbott."

"We're architects, Mr. Gold, not killers."

"That remains to be seen," said Alexander thoughtfully, "that remains to be seen."

As soon as the door closed behind Kirsch, I turned to Pearl and said, "Shut up." To Alexander I said, "You too." He understood, of course, but she needed an explanation.

"Craziness is contagious," I told her. "There is enough tension in those guys to make a healthy man sick. Alexander is not yet his former cast-iron self. He's just had two solid days of fencing with four somewhat disturbed people, any one of whom may be a murderer. So please take him for a nice relaxing walk and don't talk business."

Hopeless. So I told Alexander, "Darling, go for a nice walk with the nice lady. I'm expecting a handsome young tax-shelter salesman and I need some privacy. When you come back I'll give you an egg cream."

He was suspicious. "A real one? A Gold Super?"

"Positively not, darling. You should live so long until you taste sugar and cream from my lily-white hands. A Gold Super? Never! But a substitute, a good substitute, maybe a great substitute, that only a *maven* from *mavenland* could tell from the real thing. Go already."

The ersatz egg cream was made with powdered skim milk and artificial sweetener, but I used real vanilla seeds and a drop of almond extract. If you had never tasted a Gold Super, you would think this one very good. Not great, but potable. But if you've had nothing to eat for two months that tasted better than cardboard, you would kiss me on both cheeks. Even Pearl liked it. She gave me a grudging one star, but I noticed that she schlurped up the foam from the bottom of the glass.

XV

The next morning after breakfast, I opened the discussion. "So, Alexander, you have four possibles. All crazy, all killers in their souls. Which one?"

"Five," he answered, "not four."

"I'm excluding Jonathan."

"I'm including R.C."

"Fathers-in-law don't kill their sons-in-law. The classical shotgun is just to concentrate the mind wonderfully."

"If everyone in the office knew about Roger's attempts to reincarnate his mother by fooling around with little blonde teenagers, R.C. knew too."

"If every man who fooled around was killed by his wife's father, the population problem would vanish. Better a fooler-arounder than a widowed daughter, I always say."

"Doesn't that depend on how R.C. felt about his only daughter," asked Pearl, "and about adultery?"

"Sure," I answered, "but I don't see R.C. killing the goose that laid the golden eggs."

"All the others felt they'd eventually make more

money without Roger," she said. "Why not R.C. too?"

"All right," I gave in, "leave him on the list. But as a suspect, he is very poor quality. So who done it, Alexander?"

"I don't know," he answered. "The pattern isn't complete."

"What's left?" I asked.

"The wife. Irma Miller Talbott."

"She's the only one who loses by her husband's death," I protested. "The insurance covers less than two years' income. Besides, she couldn't have done it. She was downstairs, continuously, with Linnet Carter, for at least fifteen minutes before Roger Talbott was killed. Roger was stabbed about five minutes before the doctor saw him, just at the time Jonathan went into Roger's office. Unless the maid was bribed, and Jonathan is lying to protect Irma Talbott. Maybe he has a thing for short blond matrons." I turned to Pearl. "Here's your chance to get a change from delivery boys, doll. When you have Jonathan panting, squeeze the truth out of him."

Alexander frowned. Somehow, to him, Pearl has to be protected. I know better. These comp lit majors know all about the seamy side of life from all over the world. It's the books they read.

"Don't joke," said Alexander. "I'm sure that Jonathan was telling the truth as he saw it, which may not be the same I will see. But even if Irma Talbott is as pure as the driven snow, I'm sure she can tell me things that will help me. Look how much we learned from the architects."

"Okay," I said, "Pearl will get R.C. to bring her here."

"No," he said thoughtfully. "I want to see Talbott's studio. There has to be a way to get in and out that no one knows about. If there is, I'll find it. Arrange to meet in her home. Make sure there's something to stand on to examine the skylight. Bring a big flashlight and a Polaroid."

"Forget it, Alexander." I was firm. "That's way across town. You're not supposed to go so far from home."

"I really didn't intend sprinting all the way," he said sarcastically. "If you cross their palms with silver, charioteers will permit you to enter their conveyances."

"But what if you have a relapse?"

"Pearl and you will be with me. The house is halfway between Bellevue and Mount Sinai, with a few more hospitals and lots of doctors' offices in the vicinity. And I don't intend to climb the stairs; they have an elevator, remember?"

"He's right," said Pearl the Fink. "It'll be good for him to get away from the West Side for a while. And I'm sure it will be very helpful to see the scene of the crime. I may even get a feeling about it when I am there."

So I gave in. Besides, I also wanted to see the place where Roger Talbott was killed. Pearl isn't the only one with sensitivity and Alexander isn't the only one with brains, though neither of them would admit it. People think that a woman who is somewhat over the average in height and a little over in weight, is not only an unfeminine golem, but is slow-witted and insensitive, too. We aren't. We just act that way, sometimes. So the pain won't show.

In the dusk with the light behind her, thirty-five-year-old Irma Miller Talbott might very well have passed for twenty-three. She was small and tanned, with a model's thinness, and moved lightly with somewhat more turnout than working ballerinas used. In the harsh, unshaded glare of the very-in bare-filament bulbs which lit the ground-floor study, she was forty-five trying to pass for eighteen.

A pink ribbon tied her gold metal hair in a tight ponytail. The pullback gave her face the hard stiff shape of the newly-facelifted, but the visible play of muscle beneath the almost fatless skin of her face, and the way she held her chin high, like an aging actress, showed she had not yet drunk of that fabulous fountain.

She was wearing black opera pumps, black cocktail pajamas, and black pearls, as befitted a new widow, with only a sprinkle of sequins (black) across the top of her bosom to give a feeling of lightness and to catch, with tiny flickers, the quivering beneath the satin.

She noticed me staring at her and said, "I design all my

own clothes. A little woman comes in and drapes them for me right here in my own study."

"Remarkable," I remarked. "The design shows a skill and talent equal to some of the best-known couturiers." I had to say something before Alexander opened his mouth with a lecture on taste, but I meant the compliment exactly as worded. "Have you ever tried your hand at designing for others? I feel you could produce a line that would be the talk of the fashion world."

"Oh yes," she trilled in a voice higher than Marie Wilson's but lower than Betty Boop's, "my friends have urged me to, over and over, but I have so many interests —" she waved her hand languidly. "Time presses so. If Daddy hadn't insisted that I see you— In one hour I have a class with Mischa, then I must have my hair done by Victor. I do so adore class; strenuous exercise which adds to a woman's natural grace and beauty. You should try it yourself, Mrs. Gold," looking me up and down, "it would so add to your appearance." I noticed she carefully did not look at Pearl. The coward.

I politely did not kill her on the spot, but pulled a chair over for Alexander so he could sit directly opposite her. He would kill the little weasel for me.

He didn't. In fact, he was unnaturally polite. Alexander does not pick on the weak, the helpless, or the moronic. If he starts up with you, you've been complimented. I've been complimented many times.

"Mrs. Talbott," he said, "I sympathize with your bereavement and I will try to make this painful interview short." The big faker actually took her hand in his and held it tenderly. "I must ask you some questions about that terrible day. I hope it doesn't upset you."

"Oh no, Mr. Gold," she tweeted. "I've been through this with the police, you know. I'm much stronger than I look.

But isn't it all settled? I mean, that terrible boy—we caught him doing it. Daddy says you think he is innocent."

"It may be so, Mrs. Talbott," he answered. "I'll be grateful for any help you can give me."

"Please call me Irma," she smiled bravely. "I'll try to help in any way I can."

"Thank you, Irma." The rat can be charming if he concentrates. The only trouble is, I know that if he's charming, he 's doing it purposely. Which, when he does it to me, makes me wonder why. "I understand you brought your husband his favorite snack at ten o'clock."

"Yes. When I was home, he liked me to toast it for him. Linnet doesn't have the touch."

"Was he in good spirits when you last saw him?"

"When he was working he wasn't in any spirits; he didn't notice that I'm alive. He took one look at me and went back to work."

"Did he eat or drink while you were there?"

"No. I just put the tray on the right-hand desk so he could reach it while he was working. He liked to nibble."

"Then the Candell boy came in?"

"Yes, late. Roger was angry, I could hear it in the kitchen."

"How long was it before Candell called down?"

"Right away. A minute or two."

"Why didn't you rush upstairs?"

"I had to call the doctor. I didn't trust Linnet to do the right thing. The doctor might not have believed her if she said it was an emergency."

"You think very quickly."

"Yes. All my friends say I can always be depended upon to do the exactly right thing in case of trouble."

"How long was it before the doctor came?"

"Right away. He's only just down the block. He's our family doctor." She shuddered delicately. "He made me hold the pad on Roger's back, right on the blood. It was horrible. I almost fainted."

"But you didn't faint?"

"I'm not the fainting type; I come from good stock. Dr. Levin says that if we could have gotten Roger to the hospital soon enough, my holding the pad on the bleeding would have made all the difference in the world."

"I'm sure he was right. May I see Roger's studio?"

There wasn't room for all of us in the tiny elevator, so Beauty and The Beast went up first. He's so big—it was a tight fit and I hope he enjoyed it. Then Pearl and I went up.

It was just as described: the tiny vestibule off the elevator leading into the big white empty room; the desks at each side of the table; the lines of filing cabinets along the walls; the blank white wall opposite the drafting table; and the huge bubble skylight over the work cluster.

"I left it exactly the way it was," she said. "I haven't finalized it yet, but I'm going to make this room a museum, so that the world can see how my husband worked, the greatest living architect of all time."

"Won't that interfere with your cultural activities?" I asked.

"I don't mean now," she replied, "I mean eventually, when Daddy says it's the right time, taxwise."

"You did make some changes," Alexander said. "You cleaned the carpet."

"Well, of course. It would have been too horrible otherwise. I had it done as soon as the police allowed."

"And the drafting chair? Wasn't it further back, away from the drafting table?"

"Only a few feet. But it was this way when he was

working. That's what counts in a museum. Authenticity."

"Was anything else moved?"

"Just the chair."

He turned to me. "Norma, would you check the skylight?"

Irma darted ahead of me and tore two pieces of paper out of the drawing pad on the table and placed them for me to stand on. I thanked her silently for making sure that the table would not dirty my shoes. The screws holding the skylight in place were rusted tight and covered with dust and cobwebs. Short people would never have noticed.

I then checked the windows; same story. I went into the emergency stairway. The moment I touched one panic bolt, before I even touched the second one, a bright red light went on and a bell started ringing loudly. The bell didn't stop until I entered the stairway and closed the door firmly behind me. I climbed the iron ladder fixed to the wall to get a closer look at the roof scuttle. The sliding bolts were in place, covered with rust and real cobwebs, not glued-on ones. There was no way for me to open the door to get back in, so I knocked on the door. Pearl pushed it open, and again the bell rang and the red light flashed.

"Was everything working on that day?" Alexander asked.

"Yes. The police tested everything. The bell and the light work on each floor and in the kitchen, too."

Alexander changed the subject. "I understand that your husband spent a good deal of time here. What was he working on?"

"His books. He was doing a set of books."

"Books?" Alexander was really astounded. "I didn't know your husband wrote."

"Not written books, drawing books. Creating books."

"I don't understand."

"Well," she drew a deep breath, "you know how Johann Sebastian Bach, the great composer, wrote two great books, but not with words, *The Art of the Fugue* and *The Well-Tempered Clavier.* In *The Art of the Fugue* he showed how to write a fugue, going from the most simple to the most complicated counterpoint, with inversions and reflections and such. It was also great music as well, the greatest definitive work on counterpoint. Nothing since has come up to it.

"In *The Well-Tempered Clavier,* Johann Sebastian Bach wrote forty-eight preludes and fugues, two in each possible key, to show what could be done with a tempered keyboard, one that is tuned to sound right in any key." I could hear the flat tone of rote memorization in her voice.

"And this is what your husband was doing?" asked Alexander.

"More. Much more. He wasn't creating one book, or two, he was creating hundreds."

"On architecture?"

"Of course not. Architecture was just too easy for him. It was no challenge, no fun. He used to play with architecture once in a while, just for a change. Here, I'll show you." She pulled open the big bottom drawer of the right hand desk. It was full of blocks, plastic and wood, like children's blocks but in far greater variety. Cubes, squares, prisms, rectangles, in all sizes and proportions. And pyramids, large and small, long and short, squat and slim, more pyramids than all the other blocks together.

Irma selected a double handful and placed them on the table top. She placed several squares on top of each other in inverse size order, the smallest on bottom. Topping the stack with a pyramid, she said, "Voilà, another building.

Roger used to play with these once in a while. He would make different buildings for an hour or two and then put them away. He said if anyone wanted a building he had thousands of them in his head, all ready to make a sketch of. Architecture was so easy for him; he never took it seriously."

"Then what were his books about?" asked Alexander.

"He was the greatest artist who ever lived; the greatest draftsman. He had a perfect line. Never made a mistake, never smudged, never erased. What he drew, stayed. And never a false or wasted line. He did drawing books."

"You mean he drew? Drawings?"

"Yes, in pencil. Plain number two yellow pencil. Charcoal was for fakers who couldn't control their hands. Painting took too long, he could only turn out five or six paintings a day. Besides, the color made it too easy."

"Five paintings a day sounds like a lot," I said.

"Not for Roger. He was very fast because he knew what he was doing and he had the natural skill and talent. He didn't have to think, he knew what to do. He used to turn out fifty drawings an hour, more if he got going good."

"All out of his imagination?" asked Pearl.

"Certainly not. He would never do a thing like that. Everything he did was real, had to be real. He would go out early in the morning and sit in the park, or stand on a street corner, or in front of a store, anywhere he felt like. Then he would watch."

"Just watch? Not sketch?"

"People don't act real when they're being drawn. Even pigeons would act different when he was sketching them. They knew. So he just watched and recorded. He had perfect eyes and a perfect mind, just like a camera. In some ways, he was superhuman."

"He just watched all day long?"

"Yes. The next day he would go upstairs and draw. All day. He would look at the paper, he used only eleven-by-fourteen drawing parchment, and see the picture right on the paper. Then he would follow what he saw and draw. That's how he was so fast and accurate."

"He actually saw what he had seen the day before?"

"That's what he said, he just traced what he saw. Not only the day before, he could see whatever he wanted, once he had seen it, as clear as the day he had seen it."

"And that's why he had the white wall in front of the desk," said Alexander, excited.

"Yes," she was pleased at his comprehension. "For small parts of big things. Like if he wanted to draw one pigeon out of a flock, he'd just project the picture on the wall and pick out the pigeon he wanted and project it on the drawing pad and do it."

"Fifty pictures an hour?" I mused. "You must have thousands of drawings."

"Hundreds of thousands. They're all in the files, that's why we have so many. He's been doing it all his life. He has a book on almost anything you could think of; how to draw it under any conditions: sunlight, darkness, clouds, rain, fog, electric light, neon, anything. All perfectly accurate."

"May I see some?" Alexander asked.

She took out a folder at random. In it was a set of drawings of a doorway. They were as accurate as photographs. The lines were perfectly straight, the angles square. It was unbelievable that this was done without instruments. Not just a line drawing; the grain showed in the wood, the shadows were textured. Each drawing was slightly different from the others as the sun moved. They were signed and dated in the lower left-hand corner.

"Did he always sign and date everything?" Alexander asked.

"Not at first, but then I made him," answered Irma. "It increased the value."

"Didn't this interfere with, even clash with, your outgoing nature?" asked Pearl. "Your pattern of growth?"

"Sometimes. But I got used to it. I wouldn't want to go down in history as one who would stifle a genius. When he didn't want to go with me to a ballet, I went by myself, or with friends. I have lots of friends, you know. We never clashed, Roger always accommodated to a situation when it was important. And I would never intrude upon his space when he was working. Actually, our personalities complemented each other."

"You're a remarkable woman, Irma," said Alexander solemnly. He was so obvious I could have kicked him, but she lapped it up. "So Roger was practicing his art right up to the moment he was murdered. How very dramatic, just like an opera."

"Yes, he gave his life for his art. In the book I am going to write about him, I'm putting in a whole chapter about his last moments. With reproductions of his last drawings."

"I take it you've filed those also?"

"Of course. I wouldn't leave them out to get dirty."

"What were they on, Irma?"

"A small Korean fruitstand that just opened up on Lexington Avenue. A series that not only showed the different light, but also the different conditions. Like the store closed, the store open, the fruit put out, the fruit sold, closing up, complete."

"Wasn't he working on the General Conglomerates Building, the cathedral of business?"

"Yes. Actually, that was the drawing on his board when—when it happened."

"Didn't you give that to Mr. Kirsch to work from?"

"Oh, no, I made a Xerox. Roger's originals never leave this room. They are given to the critic who shows the greatest understanding of what Roger was trying to communicate. Sort of like a prize. Daddy insists on it, though I don't see why. Roger's originals are very valuable. Daddy insists that I give this one away too, even though it's probably worth a lot more, now that there aren't going to be any more original designs."

"So you still have the drawing here?" Alexander asked. "Would you allow me to see it?" He sounded as though he were asking for the Queen's hand in marriage.

"Well, if you promise not to touch it with your hands." Alexander nodded reverently as she put the sketch on the table and turned the lights on it.

As Erik Kirsch had said, it looked like four square-sectioned rectangular blocks on end, clustered around a fifth block which was slightly taller than the other four. On top of each block was a pyramid. That's all. From this you get rich? Yes, God help America.

The signature and date were in the lower left-hand corner. Just above were three doodles. Not doodles, really, they were very neatly drawn. A for neatness, Roger.

The lowest doodle looked like a sausage in front of a vegetable, a big radish or a thick carrot.

Above that was a cross section of something architectural, like many I had seen when Alexander was a practicing engineer. A roof, I'm sure. A concrete slab, it had the typical concrete hatching symbols, with sheetrock or something laminated to the bottom of the slab. Built-up roofing material above the slab, three plies, very clearly drawn, and thick rigid insulation above that, with gravel or crushed stone, that was clear, embedded in asphalt or pitch and protecting the insulation. Definitely a cross section of a concrete roof slab.

Above that was a first try at a cathedral. Standard front with two tall twin spires at each side, with somewhat spherical tops. Definitely a cathedral, probably a quick sketch before he did the final General Conglomerates Building drawing.

"Beautiful," Alexander whispered, full of awe. Awful. "Just beautiful. And this is what you sent to the office?"

"Exactly this. All I did was put a piece of paper over the stuff on the left before I made the copy. He had never done that before and I didn't want them to think he had lost his touch. He always drew exactly what he wanted, he never had to try out anything. Every drawing was final."

"Yes," said Alexander, "I can understand your feelings. It was a real pleasure meeting you, Irma. I hope I may have the pleasure again soon." He kissed her hand. Actually.

Pearl and I went down first. I checked my watch; thirty-nine seconds for the trip. They came down two minutes and twelve seconds later. She must have been climbing all over him. He had that stupid look on his face like when he's been sneaking chocolate bits. It was so obvious that even sensitive Pearl noticed it; I know, because she carefully didn't make a crack.

I don't mind when some dame takes a liking to my husband; it shows good taste. In certain limited areas. I don't even mind when he likes it; the filthy little beasts can't help themselves. What I do mind is when he laps it up from a phony moron—I mean a real moron who is also a phony—like Irma Talbott. And the worst part is, he thinks I am too dumb to notice. Hah! That will be the day.

"*Au revoir,* Irma," he said at the door, "*au revoir.*" If I could figure out a way to frame her, and I just might, he would see her again, all right, in the electric chair. Which, if she had her way, would be covered in glitter. With strobes.

As soon as we were seated in the taxi I told him, "I know who did it."

He didn't even blink. "Who?" he asked calmly.

"Unfortunately, it wasn't Irma Talbott," I answered. "But before I name the killer, I have to lay the foundation."

"Go ahead," he said, suspiciously gracious. Usually, in situations like this, he would tell me I was wrong before I had a chance to say anything. Now, he was letting me follow a chain of logic. I should have stopped, but I didn't know how to without losing face. Besides, I was pretty sure I was right.

"Talbott never doodled, never made false lines, right?"

"Right."

"So the doodles meant something: the name of the

killer, or at least a clue to the name. Remember how he used to give talks at his award dinners without saying a word, just sketching?"

"Why not just write the name, Norma?" asked Pearl. "It would be much quicker and surer."

"Because the killer was standing over him and would have taken the whole pad away if he saw his name or any obvious reference," answered Alexander testily. First time for Pearl. There'd be more. She'd learn.

"That was a cross section of a roof in the middle, wasn't it, Alexander?"

"Not just the roof, the whole concrete slab and the sheetrock below."

"Doesn't matter. The killer was Rufus Cornelius Miller. Roof-us."

"That's all? What about the other two clues?"

"Not important. Camouflage."

"I will not accept that," he said firmly. "They were not drawn accidently or for fun. Each sketch has a function, I am sure of that. Talbott had a knife at his back; was within seconds of death. Only a short time, one minute, to name his killer and to do it in such a way that the killer would not understand it, at least in the heat of the moment."

"How do you know he had one minute?" Pearl asked.

"Obvious." Alexander was very short with her. To paraphrase an old Pennsylvania Dutch saying, 'Blondness don't last; brains do.'

In spite of her looks, I really like Pearl, so I explained. "Talbott spoke to Candell. He was alive then. He sent the elevator down, Candell got in, went up, and there was Roger with a knife in his back. Total elapsed time, maybe one minute, thirty seconds. Both Roger and the killer had to know that."

"Couldn't that have been a tape recording of Talbott's voice?"

"Theoretically, yes; practically, no," I told her. "To tape the right words here and there, and to splice them together with exactly the right timing and inflections would be very difficult. To turn the recorder on and off at exactly the right time, or to time the pauses, would be even more difficult. What if Jonathan had spoken more hesitantly, or said different things? What if he had been earlier, or later. No, the tape is out."

"The killer could have imitated Talbott's voice, couldn't he?" She didn't know when to stop.

"What for? Take a chance that the maid or Mrs. Talbott would notice the imitation just to kill Talbott one minute earlier? We're not working with split-second schedules; nobody has an alibi except the maid and our little Golden Girl of Too Many Talents."

"I think we can all agree that Talbott was alive when he spoke to Jonathan," said Alexander. "What has the cathedral to do with R.C.?"

"Somewhere in this world there has to be a Saint Rufus. Or a Saint Cornelius. Or even a Saint Rufus Cornelius, and this is his church. Roger Talbott saw it once, or a picture of it, and filed it away in his computer memory. Or even," I had a sudden flash, "a Saint X the Miller. That has to be it. I'll research it. If it exists, I'll find it."

"What about the sausage and the carrot?" he asked.

"Two things." I was really hot now. "First, he drew a meat and a vegetable together. To show that the killer was an omnivore, that it couldn't be Jonathan, who is a strict vegetarian. Second, he didn't have time to finish the drawing. The radish wasn't a radish, it was an ear of corn. Corn-elius, right? He just didn't have time to draw in the kernels. Look at the perspective; definitely corn."

"Well, the reasoning isn't bad, but it's not too good either. How did Roger know that Jonathan was a vegetarian? Sure," he held up his hand to stop me, "he might have found out somehow, but it's pretty farfetched. And maybe the vegetable is an ear of corn which he didn't fill in. But why didn't he draw the few lines needed to indicate husks? Again, maybe no time. But what about the salami? We don't have anything to indicate scale, but whatever it is, I don't see how it fits R.C."

"Maybe Talbott knew something about R.C. that we don't know. If it's there, I'll research him down to his little pink toenails."

"I've always felt R.C. is a possible," he said, "But what we have on him would not please William of Occam."

Suddenly Pearl spoke up. "It was Bishop. Look at the clues. John Chapelle Bishop. That's the cathedral. Chapel. Close enough. And Bishop. Double check. And John. There must be a cathedral that looks like that for John the Baptist, John the Divine, John the Something. It should be easy to check out all the Johns in the Church and see if they had any cathedrals that looked like this one."

"What about the roof section?" I asked.

"A quick way to show the killer was an architect."

"But they are all architects. Even, in a sense, R.C., who is part of an architectural firm."

"To differentiate from a nonarchitect. To repeat that the killer was an architect."

"And the food?"

"That's the clincher," Pearl whispered, awed at her own understanding. "That's not real food; they're symbols. Phallic symbols. Both of them. Two male phallic symbols, denoting two males. And who is the only homosexual in the lot? Bishop. I knew he was the killer the moment I laid eyes on him. And he's the craziest of the lot."

"Well," I said, "There is some logic to that. But you're assuming that Roger knew what a phallic symbol was. From what we've learned, he was a *ne kulturni* type; probably never read a book in his life."

"Everyone knows what a phallic symbol is today," she retorted. "It's even in the papers."

"Look," said Alexander, "we can play word games all we want, but it won't get us anywhere. I'm sure there is a Saint Thomas cathedral somewhere, but unless it looks exactly like the doodle, it doesn't help. As for the roof symbol, Bauer is also an architect. And Bauer means 'farmer' in German, which takes care of the food symbol.

"Further, there has to be a Saint Erik cathedral, Erik Kirsch is an architect, and Kirsch means 'cherry' in German, so that's the food. But it's too thin, I need more."

Suddenly I felt a chill. I knew. I mean I really knew. Definitely. "Alexander," I said, putting my hand on his arm, "listen to me. Please. Don't interrupt. This is important."

His eyes opened wide. "Okay," he grunted, "talk."

"You know that new fruit store that just opened up on Broadway? With all those cute little Korean kids helping out? And that little girl on the register who is maybe eight and never makes a mistake?"

"No, I've never seen it."

"I forgot. You were in the hospital." Just then we were home. I paid the driver and didn't speak until we were in Alexander's office.

"I went into that store last week. The stuff was fresh, the prices right, and they were friendly and helpful. They had lots of vegetables I had never seen before. I bought a big order and even served one of them last week. Remember that big white radish I gave you in paper-thin slices?"

He looked suddenly alert. "It's not the same." He's always surprising me. He reads so much he knows everything, almost. But I was absolutely sure, this time.

"I know. They spell it differently every week, depending on which kid writes the sign. Sometimes it's 'taikuan' and sometimes it's 'daikon,' but the first time I saw it, it was spelled 'dakon.' That's how Talbott must have seen it when he was drawing his Korean fruit store. It's a radish, not a carrot or a phallic symbol. A Korean radish. Called 'dakon.' And the sausage isn't a salami, it's a frankfurter. A frank. Frank Dakin."

Alexander was silent, thinking.

I went on. "And if there isn't a cathedral to Saint Francis Xavier that looks like this, there has to be one to Francis of Assisi. Or some Francis. There has to be, and I'll find it."

"What about the roof section?" he asked.

"That's the best part. Not only does it say 'an architect killed me,' it specifically says who."

"What do you mean?"

"The sheetrock glued, laminated, to the bottom of the concrete, that's definitely sheetrock, isn't it?"

"It's the commonly used symbol."

"No mention of manufacturer?"

"No. The symbol is generic. It represents gypsum board, sheetrock, that's all."

"And the concrete? That's definitely the concrete symbol?"

"There's no doubt about it. Not just the standard symbol in cross section, but the proportions too."

"Does the symbol show the manufacturer?"

"Norma, stop asking foolish questions. You've been

around me long enough to know that material symbols don't show a manufacturer. Besides, there is no such thing, in the usual sense, as a manufacturer of concrete."

"The roofing, it shows three plies of membrane?"

"Clearly. He used a sharp pencil. What are you driving at?"

"The insulation over the roofing, what was the symbol?"

"Standard rigid insulation board; Fescoboard or Styrofoam or—" He stopped. He knew.

I pressed on. "And who makes Styrofoam?"

"Dow Chemical."

"Exactly. Dow Chem. Frank Dow-Chem. He's the one. By all three doodles, he's the killer." I felt triumphant. Pearl looked envious. Alexander looked thoughtful.

I had really done it; made the intuitive jump, Alexander style, but this time I did it before him. A little adulation would have been in order, not that he ever would, but it would have been nice if he did. I would have been nice about it, too, gracious, not rub his nose in it, the way he always did to me.

He finally spoke. "If he did it, Norma, how did he do it? I don't see the pattern with Dakin; it's not there. That's the problem, how did he do it?"

"I don't know that yet, Alexander. But since we know who, the technicalities will fall into place when we probe deeper. He's bound to have made some mistakes, left some clues. Now that we know where to look, we'll find them. I'll research it starting tomorrow morning. Thoroughly."

"I don't know, Norma, I don't know. I don't see it." He was inside, deep, talking more to himself than to me. "I always felt, in this case, that when I found out how it was done I would know who did it. Not the other way around. It's not complete; the pattern still isn't there."

What wasn't there was the willingness to recognize what I had done; to give me credit. He would have to, though, when I got the rest of it. As I surely would. All it needed was some high-powered digging. My specialty.

XVIII

The next morning, Pearl wanted some points clarified. "Talbott was still alive when Jonathan came into the room. He pointed at Jonathan, right?"

I answered that. "Talbott wasn't pointing at Jonathan, he was showing his left hand as if he were holding a pencil, to indicate that he had drawn the name of the murderer."

"Understood," she said. "Now, when Jonathan came into the room, it was empty. No one was there. There was no place to hide."

"Those desks at each side of the table are pretty big," I pointed out. "Dakin could have been hiding behind one of them."

"Then how did he get out? No one could have left the room while Jonathan was there. It was a bare room. Even if Jonathan were looking at the body, he would have seen movement against that white background. Where would Dakin have gone? He couldn't go down the elevator; the maid was coming up."

"True," I admitted. "What are you getting at?"

"Dakin left the room before Jonathan entered it."

"Sounds reasonable. So?"

"So Talbott was alive at his desk for at least five or ten seconds. Long enough to write the name of the murderer in plain English. Why didn't he?"

"Because the killer prevented it," Alexander answered. "He took the pencil out of Talbott's hand after he stabbed him, that's why Talbott didn't write on his shirt or his skin. Then he moved the chair, with Talbott in it, away from the table. Remember what Jonathan said? The chair was a few feet from the table."

"That proves a man did it," I said. "That took strength."

"You could have lifted him," said Pearl helpfully.

"Unfortunately I wasn't there. Both Mrs. Talbott and the maid are small."

"A woman could have dragged the chair," Alexander said. "Let's check the police photos of the carpet. Tell Burt to get me a set."

"Neither of the women could have killed him," I said. "Jonathan saw both of them downstairs before he entered the elevator."

"Agreed," said Pearl, "but we can learn something from the police photos. A strong man could have picked up the chair with Talbott in it; a weak one would have dragged it. R.C. and Dakin are both small. Bauer is big but flabby. Bishop could have lifted Talbott with one pinky. I don't care what you say about the clues, Bishop is the killer. His psychology is right."

"Bishop and the others," I replied, "are also smart enough to drag the chair purposely. Sight unseen, I'll bet a nickel that the photos show drag marks on the carpet."

"Norma is right," Alexander said. "But this leads to another point. Why take the pencil, drag away the chair? Why not stick the knife in a few more times to make sure? Cut his throat or arms, so he couldn't write? Why go to all this trouble when it could have been finished with a few more quick strokes of the knife?"

"Why a knife," Pearl jumped in, "instead of a gun? We did this before, but now it fits perfectly."

"Yes, and why then?" I asked. "It fits, too. Couldn't he have been killed five minutes earlier? An hour earlier? If the killer could get in and out so easily, why not do it without rushing, a day earlier, with plenty of time to move around without worrying about screaming maids or when Jonathan would come in? Why do it in that room at all? If the killer knew where the secret passage was, he could have killed Talbott in his sleep. After seeing Goldilocks, I'm sure they had separate bedrooms."

"Remember what I said last week?" asked Alexander. "When I knew Jonathan was innocent? Why in this house? Outside would have been easier and safer. Push him in front of a truck, stab him in a crowd; there must have been hundreds of opportunities."

"You're right, Alexander," I said, "it was all to frame Jonathan; that's the key. I'll dig into it and find which of the five crossed paths with Jonathan and that's it. It still has to be Dakin, though."

Alexander spoke thoughtfully, "You can check the intersections of all five with Jonathan, but I don't think it will be fruitful. That Jonathan was framed is clear, that's why the murder was done where, how, and when it was. But I don't see Jonathan as the target. Whoever was visiting Talbott that day, or maybe even that week, would have been the framee."

"Why couldn't Jonathan have been deliberately chosen?"

"Obvious. Someone goes to a lot of trouble to kill Talbott in this complex and risky way. Why? It would be so easy to kill him and then apologize. 'I didn't know the gun was loaded, Judge, and oh my God, I killed him!' or 'We were standing on the thirteenth-floor scaffold and my foot slipped and I fell against him and oh my God, it was all my fault.' Or any of a hundred different ways."

"Well, why didn't the killer do it accidently?"

"Because the killer had a very strong, clear, almost obvious reason to want Talbott dead; something that had happened which would have made a very deep investigation certain, which would have turned up such strong evidence that no one would believe the accident story. Maybe Talbott had run over the killer's child in St. Louis; maybe Talbott had an illegitimate son who hated him. Whatever.

"The only way to avoid that investigation was to have another person as scapegoat. That other person must have no connection with the killer. Absolutely none. If you're going to pick a fall guy, you don't pick one who can be connected to you. I'm sure the killer had no connection with Jonathan; the poor kid just happened to be there and it was lucky for the killer that Jonathan had two motives instead of one."

"What would have happened," Pearl asked, "if the next visitor to Talbott's office had no motive for killing him?"

"From what we've learned of Roger, anyone he knew would have had a motive for killing him. But if the visitor was someone who had no motive, the killer had two choices: wait for the next potential framee or frame the one who happened to be there. A bloody knife in your hand and a still-living victim at your feet is pretty strong evidence, especially in that room. But I think he would have waited."

"Could he have come the day before and stayed behind, hidden overnight, and come out to kill Talbott the next day? Then hidden again and waited to leave until the police left?"

"Hidden where?" Alexander asked. "No place in that room, not even for a midget in a filing cabinet. Talbott wouldn't allow anyone to stay behind; he didn't even allow his wife or the maid inside without him. No, the killer didn't leave anything to chance or to the hope that Talbott would act out of character. This was carefully planned; the killer knew how to get in and out at will, he knew how to appear and disappear *within* the normal, usual range of Talbott's activities. I'm sure he disappeared, not only before the police arrived, but before Jonathan came into the room."

There was a pause, then Pearl asked, "How did he disappear? How did he appear in the first place?"

"I don't know," he choked out. I could have cut Pearl's tongue off. "It's never taken me so long to solve any puzzle. I lost brain cells, I know it. Maybe if I had more pieces, I could fit it all together."

"Which pieces?" I asked foolishly, just to say something, to get his mind off the missing brain cells.

"How should I know?" he replied testily. "If I knew which pieces, I'd know what they are. I want more interviews."

"Who?" I asked.

"You take the doctor and Pearl gets the girl Kirsch

saw jogging in the Park. Burt can find out her address."

So Pearl was promoted from assistant drudge to private eye. Big deal. That much farther to fall when she messes up.

Dr. Calvin Levin was gray, skinny, sour, and busy. The only way I could see him on such short notice was to ride with him to Mt. Sinai when he went to visit his patients. Traffic was heavy but the trip was short, so we got right down to business.

"When I got the call that he had been stabbed," he said, "I grabbed my bag and my emergency bag—I always keep a special trauma bag handy, what with all the muggings and the heart attacks—and told my nurse to call an ambulance, private, you could die of old age trying to get a nine-one-one and the hospitals aren't any better, and I ran."

"How long between the time you got the call and the time you got to Talbott," I asked.

"A minute or two. I move pretty fast, keep in shape, not like some people I know. It took longer for that little elevator to creep up than for me to get to the house."

"What did you do when you saw Talbott?"

"Had to make a decision, quick. Morphine, to relax the patient, or no morphine because his breathing was very shallow."

"He was alive when you got there?"

"No question of that. But for all practical purposes, dead. If we had been right at a Trauma Center, or even an Emergency Room, I might have saved him."

"But you did try."

"We always try. I decided no morphine. I put a reflective blanket over him and pressed a pad to the wound. Mrs. Talbott held it. I cut down a vein and gave him five-hundred cc's of Ringer's Solution. He must have been bleeding badly internally and he needed the fluid volume. Then I gave him oxygen; I carry a flask and a mask in my kit."

"Then what did you do?"

"What could I do? Waited for the ambulance. Checked his heart and other vital signs."

"Was he still alive when the ambulance came?"

"I think I heard a heartbeat just before, so he probably was, but only technically."

"If the ambulance had come one minute earlier, or two, could he have been saved?"

"Doubtful. He was in his late forties and had led a sedentary life. His heart was not prepared for a major insult. The brain starts going after about four minutes, you know."

I knew, and I wished there was a way to wipe it off the tape before Alexander played it, but there wasn't. "How long before you first saw him would you say he had been stabbed?"

"Well, figuring it took me about two minutes—"

I interrupted him. "Not that way. I don't want you to reconstruct what must have happened. Just from the medical evidence."

"Young lady, medicine is not magic; we form our opinions by considering all known factors."

"How long, doctor?"

"Oh, about three or four minutes. Maybe five."

"Could it have been six or seven minutes?"

"It's possible. Depends on a lot of things."

"Eight minutes?"

"Stop that, now," he barked. "Don't start with those stupid lawyers' tricks on me. If it could have been eight, could it have been nine? If it could have been nine, could it have been ten? And before you know it, it could have been an hour. It doesn't work that way. If I say five minutes, that's a reasonable estimate. Six is possible, but the probability is lower. And it's not a straight-line graph. Ten minutes is barely possible, but it would be unusual, say a hundred-to-one against."

I changed the subject. "You're an internist, aren't you, Dr. Levin?"

"Internist is a fancy name for a general practitioner. That's me, last of a dying breed."

"You saw the Talbotts regularly?"

"Mrs. Talbott made sure they had semiannual checkups. Not for her, she's as healthy as a horse; he could have used more exercise."

"Did they have any unusual problems? Ones you couldn't handle yourself?"

He grew stiff. "Young lady, I know my limits. If any of my patients had a problem I felt I was not qualified to handle, I would send him to a proper specialist; to a brother physician." And he laughed, "ha, ha, ha" with the dry forced sound of the absolutely humorless.

We reached the hospital and I got out. Something was there in what he said, I smelled it. So instead of going right home, I went into the lobby and sat in a corner. I plugged in the recorder earphone and replayed our little talk.

Pearl had gotten home first. Naturally, she had had the easier job. She had been so overwhelmed by the promotion and her first assignment that she had forgotten to turn on her tape recorder. Alexander had been discussing this with her, I could tell. At length. Assuming that he had been ten times gentler with her than he had ever been with me, it still had to be the baddest quarter hour she had ever spent in her life. I almost took pity on her, but wothehell, Archie, you're in the big leagues now.

Finally Alexander stopped with the negative reinforcement and got specific. "How did she know it was Kirsch?"

"By his clothes," Pearl answered, like an idiot. "He always wore purple and gold. Everything. His sweatsuit, his shoes, headband, everything."

Alexander looked at her unbelievingly. "By his clothes?"

"No, no," Pearl was almost crying, "that was just in the distance. She saw his face clearly when they passed. She even smiled at him because she wanted to meet him."

"How did she know who he was?" Alexander looked at me as though I was the one who gave her the assignment.

"I asked her that," Pearl was relieved. "She didn't know him, except from seeing him jogging. The police showed her pictures and she picked him out. Later they had her identify him through a two-way mirror."

"Why isn't she jogging in the park any more?"

"Her new boy friend doesn't like jogging."

Alexander gave up and put my tape in the machine. He

played it through twice. "Did you catch that last part?" he asked. "About the specialist?"

"Of course," I replied. "I figured that a sourpuss like him doesn't know from jokes, so I dug into it. Not just Mount Sinai, but Bellevue, too. You'd be surprised how many brother physicians there are in the area: Levines, Levens, Levitskys, Leventhals, you name them."

"What about the professional societies? The specialists' groups?"

"Don't teach the cat how to drink milk," I chided, "you're talking to a professional. After what I saw of Blondie and heard about the genius architect, I knew what to do. I called the Fertility Diagnostic Center and the Fertility Research Foundation. There are three on the East Side with the right names.

"Dr. Levine and Dr. Levinson are 'we have no patients by that name.' Dr. Levitt 'does not give out information about our patients.' So now we know that at least one of them has a fertility problem. Since the Blond Bombshell is as 'healthy as a horse,' it has to be Roger who is the reason for the big empty house and Irma's endless activities."

"Excellent," he beamed, "that's exactly the way I would have done it."

Did you hear that? Exactly the way he would have done it? God's highest compliment to a mere mortal? My very first Gold Star from Alexander?

"What did you find out after that?" he asked.

"After what?" I dropped down fast. "I came right home to tell you about it. I figured it all out by myself and I checked it and I was right. What's wrong with that?"

"Nothing's wrong with it. I just—"

I cut him off, steaming. "You're always doing this to me, Alexander. First you tell me that I'm right, then you tell me I'm wrong. You pat me with one hand and slap me with the other. Don't do this to me, Alexander, my nerves are shot. I've just gone through—with you—"

"But I only asked—"

"I don't care what you asked. You shouldn't have asked anything. I did something perfectly, you said so yourself, couldn't you leave it at that? Let me enjoy being right in your eyes just once. Please, Alexander, just once." I was crying.

He stood up and put his arms around me. "Yes, yes, darling," he said, "don't cry. You've done very well. I didn't realize how much I've been asking of you, chasing you around all day. I really appreciate all you've done. Go into the kitchen and make some cocoa for both of us. I'll ask Burt to take care of one little detail and I'll be right in."

He dialed and I heard him say, "Burt, I need someone. Information. From Blue Cross. And a bank. That's all. Okay, I will when he calls me."

Pearl sensibly had slipped out earlier.

We both felt better after the cocoa, even cocoa made with skim milk and sweetener. I led him back into the office and made him sit in the recliner, upright but with his feet out. Then I sat in his lap and leaned against him, on the right side so as not to put pressure on the heart. I could hear it beat; it sounded firm and strong.

"Darling," he said contritely, "I'm sorry I criticized you. It's because I'm worried about the case. The trial is next month, and I'm no nearer to figuring out how it was done than when I started. I've been thinking, maybe I should drop the detective business and go back to engineering. I haven't brought in any income for two months. How much money do we have left?"

"Don't you worry about that. It's my job to take care of

the bank account, you just take care of getting well. When you solve the case we'll be rich. I know you'll do it; you've never failed me yet."

He still looked worried. "It's never taken me this long to solve any problem before. I lost some brain cells, I know it."

"Darling, you're just as smart as you ever were. I see it and so does everyone else. You're the greatest. Hold me and close your eyes."

I put my head on his massive shoulder and he put his huge arms around me. He felt so strong and I was safe. We slept that way the whole night, the first time we'd been together since the attack. It felt good. It felt right again.

I woke up early, a little stiff, but relaxed. I was concerned that my weight on Alexander's thighs might have compressed some blood vessels, but his muscles are so big and strong that he didn't notice any problems. He woke up early too, smiling. That never happens; he likes to sleep late.

He had a surprised look on his face. When I asked why, he said, "I know how he did it. Obvious. I should have seen it before."

"See," I said, "sleeping with me works wonders. You should do it more often. All you had to do was relax and let your subconscious take over. What about the stuff you asked Burton for?"

"I don't really need it. Useful as corroboration, but I know what it will be. And now that I know how, I know who."

"Okay, stop torturing me. Who did it and how?"

He hesitated. "Norma, please don't be offended, but I'm not going to tell you. I'm not worried that you'll talk, but if you know, it will show. Pearl will sense it, she's very sensitive (Again with the sensitive?) and she'll tell Burt. Burt's first duty is to his client, and I don't want anyone to know I know."

"Why not?"

"I can't prove anything. I don't know if I'll ever be able to prove anything. It's just a long line of reasoning, not the kind of stuff that would stand up in court. If the killer gets the slightest inkling that I know, I'll never have a chance to get him near a court. We make nothing for getting Jonathan off, we only get the rewards for information leading to the arrest and conviction of the killer. And we only make a percentage if the killer is a beneficiary."

"Is he?"

"I don't even want to discuss that with you; don't ask me again. I have to figure out how to nail the killer so it will hold up in court."

"Is there anything else you want me to do?"

"Yes. Sleep with me in our own bed tonight."

"Is that a proposition?"

"I hope so. I'll call Myron after ten and find out."

I knew what Myron would say; I'd already discussed it with him. After going over exertion and positions, he had told me, "Six weeks is what I always tell them. When they call to ask if it's okay, I know it's okay and I always say yes."

Good thinking, Myron!

It took two days, then there was a flurry of activity. Alexander had me get a video camera built into a corner of his office behind the desk, its wide-angle lens covering the room. He shifted his desk so that it was tight in the corner against the front wall and the vestibule, and placed his chair in front of the desk facing into the room. A hole was cut in the back wall, and a two-way mirror installed, as well as a screened opening so you could listen from the back room as well as see. "That's for the stenographer," he told me.

We brought in twelve straight chairs and arranged them against the walls so the camera could scan them all. A big package came, which Alexander wouldn't let me open. Later, a big lumpy bag appeared on his desk, again, not to be touched.

It was Burton's job to arrange that all the people came, each at the right time. Pearl and I were the hostesses who would very casually seat each person in the proper place.

To the right of the door, Alexander. To the left of the door, on the same wall separating the hall from the office, I sat, with Pearl on my left. We each had a steno notebook in case we sensitively noticed something. Mine, it was made clear, was for show.

On the left wall, Detective Lt. Warshafsky, the officer in charge of the case, and after him, the two insurance company representatives.

To Alexander's right, under the high windows facing the street, Burton and Mrs. Talbott. On the far wall, facing Alexander, the five suspects in order of seniority from right to left: R.C., Bauer, Bishop, Dakin, and Kirsch.

Miss Karrol, the legal stenotypist, was in the room next door where she could hear and see everything.

The nonsuspects came in early to take their seats, so there would be a lessened tendency for the architects to sit in the wrong places. The Blond Menace arrived immediately after the first insurance man. Black jeans, very tight; high black boots, very worn (sandpaper?); black peasant blouse, embroidered in red and white, very sheer, nothing underneath; a small black cowboy-type hat with a three-inch veil in front (mourning?). Alexander tried not to stare. He failed.

Bishop and Dakin came in almost together, not talking. Bishop was dressed in solid cream from top to bottom, looking beautiful and edible, like a poison toadstool. Dakin wore a casual sport shirt, blazer, and slacks, in different blues, and looked even more tense than when we first met him. A minute later Kirsch bounded in, flashing in his purple and gold sweatsuit, shoes, and headband, face red, but not breathing hard. Right behind him was R.C., in a light, carefully cut but wrinkled washable summer suit and tie. Last by several minutes was Tom Bauer, big and rumpled in a red polo shirt and gray slacks.

Alexander welcomed them all and introduced Burton as Candell's attorney. When he introduced Lt. Warshafsky, who wore a standard navy blue suit, there was a noticeable stir along the suspects' wall.

The lieutenant, who looked too young to hold that position, arose. "I am here by invitation. As far as the police are concerned, you are people who were invited to hear what Mr. Gold has to say. If you wish to leave, leave. If you wish to stay, stay. If you wish to talk, or remain silent, or call your lawyer or take any legal action, please do so.

"Mr. Gold has informed me that he has some ideas concerning the Talbott homicide, and that he will present these ideas to all of you here with me present. This is not the way I work, but I can't force him to talk to me privately unless I believe he has evidence or information useful to the investigation. I have no such belief. He also said that the real perpetrator of the homicide is in this room. I have no reason to believe that either, but if that is the case, please talk to me. I assure you that you will be treated properly and given all the rights required by law. As an example of how we observe this, let me read you what every police officer must read to a person on arresting that person."

He then read them the Miranda warning. Very neat. Without actually doing it, he did it, and now no one in the room could claim he or she was not warned. And he added to the psychological pressure. Lieutenant Warshafsky would bear cultivating.

Alexander stood up and announced, "For my part, anyone wishing to leave, now or later, is free to do so. Of course, it would be just as foolish to leave as not to have come. That would be like taking an ad in the papers saying, 'I am the real killer; investigate me in depth.' You and I both know that if the police investigated you all the way back, they would find all the evidence needed to convict you. The purpose of killing Talbott in that complicated and risky way was to build up such a strong case of circumstantial evidence that Candell was the murderer that the police would look no further. Which, being understaffed, they did."

Alexander stared at each of the architects in turn. "Why was it so important to have someone to frame? Because something happened in the past, and something was going to happen in the future, which points directly to the killer. This may be subject to change now, but if it is, other things must come out. Without a scapegoat, the killer was doomed.

"But right now, the killer *is* doomed. Just by having this meeting, I may arouse Lieutenant Warshafsky to investigate further along the lines I will discuss. If the police check you," his finger swept accusingly across the five architects, "you know you will be found out. Make it easy on yourself. Here's a phone, call your lawyer; you may get away with as little as eight years' time served."

There was silence, all eyes fixed on Alexander. He went on. "The murder. Talbott tells Candell to come up and pushes the button which frees the elevator to bring Candell up to the fourth floor.

"The killer suddenly appears behind Talbott and

presses the knife lightly into his back. He tells Talbott what he has been aching to tell him for years, while keeping an eye on the sweep second hand of his watch and listening carefully for the sound of the elevator. After sixty seconds he stops talking. When he hears the elevator, he pushes the knife in, pulls the chair away so Talbott can't reach the drafting table, takes away Talbott's pencil, glances at the drawing on the table, and disappears. Candell pushes open the vestibule door, walks in, pulls out the knife, and, presto, the police have the killer."

Lieutenant Warshafsky spoke up wearily, "Haven't you skipped a few things, Mr. Gold?"

"Sure, but I'll cover them all. Just look at the faces of my five suspects. See R.C., who knew what a failure Roger was as a husband for his beloved daughter; who knew that Roger was persistently unfaithful to her with teenage girls; who dreaded the scandal when Roger would be caught with a fourteen-year-old who screamed rape; who knew that Roger was the cause of the possible dissolution of the company he built up and loves. Don't look at your daughter, R.C., she knew about it long before you did. And let's not forget money. You're rich, but no one can ever be too rich. You know that Roger wasn't worth one percent, much less fifty percent. And you all know," his eyes swept the other four, "that you will each make more money without him, soon."

R.C. spoke up, calmly, "Mr. Gold, I did not come here to be harassed, and I will not be intimidated, nor will my daughter or my associates. If you had any real evidence that one of us was involved, you would have given it to the police. It seems to me that you're just fishing, and I have nothing more to say to you." He turned to his colleagues, "I suggest that you ignore what he says. When he is done, we will just get up and leave."

Alexander smiled, and continued. "Thomas Bauer. Money, of course. But jealousy, too. You're the one who made the first design that brought him fame. What did it bring you? You're the one who was the whole firm for those first years in Missouri. For five percent? You made him the greatest architect who ever lived, with your designs and your work. Who knows your name? Your wife wrote the first article that started everything; did anyone say thank you?"

Bauer glanced at R.C., clamped his lips together, and said nothing. His face was a deep red and his neck swelled.

"John Bishop. You're the core of the firm. He had fifty percent; you ten. If money is the measure of success, was he five times the man you are? You run the most efficient drafting room in the business; did he ever say a word of appreciation? Did he even know what you were doing? Could it have been done at all without you? And his perversion with little girls; doesn't that disgust you? What will the new firm be named? Will it be Bauer, Bishop, Dakin, and Kirsch? Or will it be Bishop, Dakin, and Kirsch? Bauer is ready to be bought out; you're rich, he's replaceable."

Bishop smiled, amused. "I haven't been so entertained in years, Mr. Gold. Everything you said so far is absolutely true. Keep it up. If you give Bauer a stroke, I won't have to buy him out."

Alexander turned to Dakin. "Frances Xavier Dakin. Service to God is your life, architecture the means. You don't mind that Talbott didn't know or appreciate your work, but you do mind that he stole your money. Money you would have given to further God's work; money he didn't earn, didn't deserve. You could have quintupled the money you gave to the Church with your extra share after his death. And he was Evil incarnate. Think of what he did to your eldest daughter."

Dakin was trembling so, I was afraid he would attack Alexander. I tensed to jump up to protect him. Kirsch placed his hand over Dakin's firmly, comfortingly. "Relax, Frank," Erik said, "he's trying to get a rise out of you." Dakin remained seated and glared at Alexander from his sunken blue eyes.

"Erik Kirsch," Alexander continued. "You're the real design genius. Everyone in the firm knows it, even R.C. A few people in the profession know it too, but not many. How does it feel to hear Talbott called the greatest architect of all time? A man who isn't even an architect? Who not only knows nothing about architecture, but doesn't even like it? Who made your life miserable with his stupid little sketches that you have to turn into real buildings? A man who took your skill and talent and claimed it as his own? How did it feel that he was ten times as rich as you are? That he has a beautiful and talented wife and you live alone? How do you like the pyramids, the endless pyramids, the childish pyramids made from little toy blocks, that win praise, fame, and the awards that should be yours?"

Kirsch closed his eyes and put his palms together. He took three slow, deep breaths and relaxed visibly. "I hope you're taping this," he said, opening his eyes, "I could use the flattering publicity."

"No denials?" Alexander asked. "No screams? You all hated him? You each had a motive to kill him?"

R.C. started to say something, then changed his mind.

Alexander loves this, I know, when he is right and someone else is dead wrong and won't admit it. He'll hammer the poor simp with logic, pound with reason, emotion, appeals to God, anything. They'll crack under the siege. It's not just his mind, it's the power of his personality, his voice like a bullet. It happened to me once; I will never let it happen again. If I'm clearly wrong, I'll say so immediately. He'll stop on a dime. It's the only way. I pity poor Dakin. If he had any sense, he'd confess right now.

But if Alexander really knew who the killer was, if he really had the evidence, why was he doing this? Did he really know? Had he lied to me, to make me feel good temporarily? Or did he want my feeling of confidence to transmit itself to the killer, to break his will?

XXII

"So," said Alexander, "back to the scene of the crime. The elevator door opens and the killer disappears. Not really. He just walks quickly to the emergency stairway exit door, opens it, goes through, closes it, and walks quietly down to the second floor. Even if Jonathan had bounded into the little elevator vestibule, even if his attention were not focused on Talbott and the blood, he wouldn't have seen the killer with the vestibule door blocking his view. Or heard him; thick carpet, you know."

Warshafsky interrupted, wearily. "Why didn't the bells ring and the lights flash? Candell stated that the switch was closed when he went to the intercom. Only Talbott's fingerprint, clear, was on the switch button. No one could have turned it off without smearing it."

Alexander was ready. "Because when the killer entered the house at the ground-floor level, he first went down the back service stair into the cellar and snapped off the circuit breaker for the alarm circuit, the one Talbott had installed when the reporter sneaked into his studio."

"How did he know which one it was?"

"I presume there was a list card on the circuit breaker panel door; there usually is. Or maybe the killer tried it out sometime before. Since no one ever used that door anyway, who would know? Of course, before he left the house, the killer snapped on the breaker again, so when the doctor opened the door, everything was working perfectly. No one could ever tell it had been off."

"How is it," Warshafsky asked, "that Talbott wasn't aware that his elaborate alarm system could be switched off so easily? Wouldn't an architect have known?"

"If Talbott were a real architect, certainly he would have known. But he wasn't a real architect. Clearly, Talbott never told the contractor who installed the alarm system to protect it against people *in* the house who knew how electrical systems worked and who could get into the electrical meter room in the cellar. So it was obvious to me that the killer was an architect, or someone who knew building construction, or, at least, someone who knew what a circuit breaker was and could gain entry to the house.

Alexander paused again. "Anyone want coffee? Tea?

Lemonade? I know it's hot in here, the air conditioning isn't designed for so many people, but to paraphrase an old Heifetz joke, it's only hot for killers. Let's see, who is sweating?" He looked at the five architects. They all were, Bauer the most. If Alexander had looked at me, I could have been included in the category.

"So now we know how the killer escaped. Down the stairs to the second floor. Wait for Linnet Carter to go upstairs. Down to the cellar to turn on the alarm system. Up to the ground floor and out the doors, locking them behind him, and into the street. Simple. Now all we need to know is how he got in."

"Yes, Mr. Gold," said the lieutenant, "how did he get in?"

"With the keys, of course, through the ground-floor entrance, while the two women were on the first floor. Five keys, but that's no problem. Keys are easy to get if you're determined and have access and time. Maybe they were lying around once when he was visiting the house or Talbott's studio, and he took impressions. Maybe someone gave them to him. The maid? Bribed? Mrs. Talbott herself? 'Do me a favor, kind sir, and drop these packages off for me at the house. I'm late, here are the keys.' Even Talbott himself. Maybe he wanted a package or a sketch picked up from the house. After all, the killer was one of his associates. No matter. The killer had the keys and he used them to get in and to lock up on the way out.

"So now we have the killer in the house, on the ground floor. He's got to get to the top floor. If he can get past the two women on the first floor, if he can get to the upper stairs, when he opens the emergency exit doors, the alarms will not go off. But how does he open these doors?

There is no hardware, no handles, nothing on the up sides of the doors, only panic bolts on the down sides. Did he disable the panic bolts the last time he was there? Very difficult. No one is allowed on that floor unless Roger is there. Also, it would be impossible to restore the situation in the two seconds he has left to get out of the studio. These are delicate alarms; if the bolts are not seated perfectly in their strikes, the alarm goes off. Gimmicking is theoretically possible, but it would take too much time to do and undo.

"Besides, how do you get from the ground floor to the third floor without being seen? The two women are in the kitchen. Is he sure they will be in the kitchen when he walks up the stairs to the first floor? Is the kitchen door open? Which way are they looking? When is Roger going to call down for coffee? If he calls ten seconds later will the killer be seen? Is Roger's watch perfectly synchronized with the killer's? When is Jonathan going to ring the bell? No, the stairs are out. Too many risks for this careful planner, too many wild cards.

"On the other hand, the elevator poses certain problems, too. There is no way the elevator will go to Roger's floor without Roger's pressing the release button. So even if the killer could call the elevator down to the ground floor without either of the two women noticing, he couldn't take it to Talbott's floor. Maybe Talbott wanted him to come up. Why? To be in at the meeting with Candell? Then why not use the front door? Maybe he could take the elevator to the floor below Talbott's, but then there is the same problem with the stairs; he can't get in through the emergency-exit doors. So what is the poor fellow to do?"

Alexander paused dramatically; hammed it up, actually. "Simple," he said. "The killer takes the elevator."

XXIII

Alexander put on his most professorial manner. "There were two opportunities for the killer to go up in the elevator: when Jonathan Candell went up, and when Irma Talbott went up with the coffee."

She jumped up. Her face wasn't hard anymore and her voice was different, softer, more like a young girl's, with a strong midwestern accent. "I didn't! He made me! He said I had to help him. I didn't know he was going to kill Roger. It was all his idea." She was hysterical. Her father tried to pull her down in her seat.

"Shut up, Irma," said Erik Kirsch firmly. "He doesn't have a damn thing. Just keep your mouth shut."

"He's right, Irma," Alexander agreed, "keep your mouth shut. I don't need any help from you. And you weren't forced to do anything. You're an accessory before, during, and after the fact. You had your chance and you were willing to let a poor innocent boy take the rap for you."

"Daddy, Daddy, help me!" She turned to R.C., sobbing. He held her and made soothing noises.

Alexander was angry. "Help you? You killed your husband, planned it for months. You're thirty-five years old, take responsibility for your actions. Your daddy can't help you, only you can help yourself."

R.C. looked up. "You're wrong there, Mr. Gold. I don't care how old she is, she's still my little girl. If there's a way to help her, I'll help her. And there'll be a way, you can bet on that."

"R.C.," Alexander conceded, "you may be right. In your place, I'd do the same. And if you follow my lead, I just might show you the way. Be patient and listen carefully."

"It was Irma's function to keep Linnet Carter on the first floor until Candell arrived, and then to send her up to Roger's studio after Candell went up, so that she could bear witness that Candell was in the room with the murdered man while he was still alive. If Jonathan had not called down on the intercom, or if Roger had not asked for another snack to be sent up, Irma would have sent the maid up with a snack anyway. Clear?"

Warshafsky nodded.

"An additional reason for sending the maid up to the studio was to give the killer a chance to get past the first floor, without being seen, so he could get back into the cellar to turn on the emergency-stair alarm again."

Warshafsky nodded again and motioned for Alexander to go on.

"Once I knew how it was done," Alexander said, "It was obvious who the killer was."

"Obvious?" Warshafsky looked puzzled.

"Crystal clear, Lieutenant," Alexander replied. "When I knew that Irma Talbott had taken the killer up in the elevator, and given him a set of keys by the way, he shouldn't have to get them the hard way, the question was, Why would she want her husband killed? Money?

True, she thought she would get a big lump if he died, but he was bringing in plenty alive. Revenge? Hate? He interfered with her freedom? Obviously not. It had to be love, sex, something like that.

"Now, let's look at it from the viewpoint of the suspects. Even if R.C. wanted to kill his son-in-law, would he involve his daughter? What about Bauer? I can't quite see him as Irma's secret lover. Or as a devious killer. His solution would be to sell out, retire to a small town, and be an architect again. Bishop? As Irma's lover? Somewhat improbable. Dakin? Break two Commandments at once? He'd sooner burn down Saint Patrick's. Erik? Yes, yes, and yes. And once I knew it was Erik, everything fell into place."

"You're right, Mr. Gold," said Warshafsky sarcastically, "it was obvious."

Alexander ignored the lieutenant. He paused for a moment, then spoke. "Kirsch was waiting in the cellar. Didn't matter how long; if things went off schedule he could come back the next time there was a visitor. When Irma Talbott took the elevator up with her husband's snack, she first went down to the cellar and picked up Kirsch. When she left the fourth floor, Erik stayed behind in the little vestibule waiting for Jonathan to arrive. Talbott never turned his head, nor could he have seen Kirsch if he had, since the vestibule door was almost closed. When Kirsch saw Talbott push the elevator-release button, he walked in on the soft white carpet, and we know the rest."

"How did he get to the house without being seen, Mr. Gold?" asked Warshafsky. "Wasn't he taking a big risk being seen? A purple and gold suit is a little obvious."

"He *was* seen, Lieutenant, by many people. But his clothes were not distinctive, except in one way. It was a hot, humid summer day. The girl who smiled at him in the park was wearing short shorts and a thin shirt. She was soaking wet. Kirsch was wearing a full sweatsuit. Why? He doesn't own lighter clothing? He's too fat and is trying to reduce? So why did he wear a heavy sweatsuit in ninety-degree heat? Because there's no way to hide a big knife in a pair of jogging shorts. Not to mention the penlight for turning off the circuit breaker. Plus a holster for the knife, it shouldn't fall out from jogging. Plus gloves for the fingerprints. And keys. Money for emergencies. Mirror sunglasses, a peaked cap, and maybe a small mustache. Most important of all, a thin plastic sweat-it-off type coverall jacket and pants, with stick-on plastic color patches for the shoes. It takes space. Not much, but you can't hide it in your T-shirt."

"Wouldn't all that make a big bulge?" asked Warshafsky.

"It could all be packed in a small flat parcel, which could not be seen through a loose bulky sweatshirt. I would guess it was taped to his chest, knife holster and all."

"That's how I would have done it," Warshafsky agreed.

"So in the park, at Talbott's street, behind a tree, in thirty seconds, no more purple and gold, presto, a new man. Who's to see? And if anyone sees, so what? No one is looking for a clothes changer. You've already caught the killer red-handed."

"Couldn't someone have seen him entering the house?"

"He probably was seen by several people, but who sees a jogger? They're invisible men. And if someone does see a jogger turn into a front yard, again so what? In one second, he's gone, under the stair. You had the killer, did you look for anyone else, Lieutenant?"

"Not really. As you said, we're understaffed."

"He did the same, opposite, on the way back. Dump the plastic suit in a garbage can. Drop the penlite and the gloves in the park. Keys down a sewer. Feed the mustache to a squirrel. Cut the holster into little pieces and flush down a public toilet. Where's the evidence?"

"Where, indeed, Mr. Gold?" asked the lieutenant, with a worried glance at Kirsch, who was sitting relaxed and smiling.

"Oh, there's evidence, all right. I'll give you some, the rest you'll have to dig for. For instance, our lovebirds were too smart to meet at her place or his, so somewhere in between you'll find their hideaway. Flash a few pictures around; your men are good at that."

"We'll do that, Mr. Gold."

"Not evidence, really, but the girl in Central Park, the jogger. From the way Kirsch described her, I would have stopped for her on the way to open-heart surgery. She even smiled at him. He didn't stop? Even to say 'Hello, what's your name and number?' He was tense? Something on his mind, maybe, that he couldn't spare two minutes? Maybe that was the one day he couldn't stop, otherwise he'd be late for a murder."

"That's not much as evidence, Mr. Gold."

"I know. It just helps to bind things together." Alexander looked at Kirsch. "You should have stopped and talked to the girl, Erik. It would have saved your life." Kirsch didn't answer.

"What's the motive, Mr. Gold?" asked the lieutenant. "We have a possible means and a possible opportunity. I need a motive."

"Sex and money," said Alexander. "Plus what I said before: jealousy, frustration, pride, and, probably, love of architecture. I feel that Talbott's designs, and his open contempt for architecture were the deciding factors, without which Erik might not have killed Talbott." Alexander addressed Kirsch. "You have the best criminal lawyer in America in this room. Take a bow, Burton. As soon as you confess, he can drop Candell and take you on as a client. Confess and claim that you did it to save American architecture."

Kirsch looked at Burton appraisingly. Alexander turned to Burton and said, "What do you think of the idea, Counsellor? Erik killed Talbott because Talbott was a rotten architect?"

"*Pro bono publico?* It's certainly a novel defense," said Burton, "but it could be dangerous. If I won the case it might mean open season on lawyers."

"Or even engineers," said Alexander. "Good point, Burt." Kirsch seemed to be weighing his decision, then he sat back, relaxed, and smiled confidently. Alexander waited a moment more, then spoke again. "Well, since Erik won't confess, let's go on with the analysis."

"It all started when they were in Europe," he continued. "Aside from not being interested in women, Bishop has a very low opinion of Irma Talbott. Plus he's in Salzburg. Roger is off somewhere staring at pigeons. Irma is alone: young, attractive, lonely. So is Erik. Munich is a romantic city, lots of things to see and do. Bang, they discover each other. They're in love and being in Europe, they probably were careless. You could trace them, Lieutenant."

"Not important, except as background. I wouldn't waste the plane fare."

"How's this? When they move to New York, Irma is twenty-seven. Basically a nice simple girl, she wants a family. Children. Roger doesn't mind. For four years they try and fail. Finally, kindly Dr. Levin sends them to kindly Dr. Levitt, the fertility wonder-worker. The lab says Irma is highly fertile, Roger is not. Three years of treatment; no results. This you can check without spending any of the department's funds; the company medical insurance pays for it. Good?"

"Nothing special yet, for a murder case. Mr. Gold."

"Now comes the good part. Irma goes to Erik. Why don't we get married? Erik thinks, why not indeed? He's tired of being the back-room boy. He wants to be the greatest architect in the world. And the boss. And very rich. And famous. And if he's not in love with Irma, he's very, very fond of her. And, and, and, and. What if Roger were dead? Two million in keyman insurance is there to fill the firm's coffers. Plus another two in widow's-buyout insurance. But suppose she doesn't sell her equity? Her fifty percent plus Erik's ten equals sixty percent. Now it will be Erik Kirsch Associates. It wouldn't cost him a penny to buy out Bauer's ten percent and sell five percent each to Bishop and Dakin at cost, to keep them quiet. R.C. can stay; Irma will inherit his ten percent soon, plus everything else he has. Neat? And Erik still owns sixty percent of the unspent four million insurance."

"That's beginning to sound like a motive," Warshafsky said.

"That's not all. Irma collects another two million on Roger's personal life insurance. Starve, they won't. But there's more. Only Irma knows what Roger is doing when he's not chasing teenage blondes. He is drawing. Fastest draw in the West. And he's real good at it, I've seen his work. Perfect likeness, like a camera. Turns out hundreds of drawings a day. In the files are about three hundred thousand drawings. He won't sell any, that's not why he's drawing.

"Six years ago, one of his architectural sketches sold for ten thousand dollars. What's it worth now, with inflation?

Plus he's a dead artist, double that figure. Don't. Stick with ten thousand. Multiply by three hundred thousand. You know how much that is? Three billion dollars. Check it; three billion! Right there on the top floor. Let's be conservative; not ten thousand, make it one thousand each. Still, three-hundred million. Is that a motive?"

"Could be. Keep talking."

"Only the stupid little blonde doesn't know some things. First, the sketches are her husband's, not hers, not even community property. Signed and dated by him. And the IRS likes to collect inheritance taxes. What's the tax on three billion? Don't bother; too much. If that's how the IRS figures it, you're in hock for the rest of your great-grandchildren's lives. The IRS uses the last sale as a basis. So they take everything. You are wiped out merely by inheriting some art. Could you give them half the drawings? Sixty percent? The IRS takes only cash. In France you can now give the tax collector his blood money in art, at his appraisal of course. Not here.

"But Talbott's architectural drawing sold for ten thousand because it was an architectural drawing by the greatest architect of all time. A curio. A one-of-a-kind. A Dürer or a Rembrandt sketch will sell for big money; they are artists, great artists. Their drawings had merit, showed beauty, an artist's hand and an artist's eye. And there aren't three-hundred thousand of them floating around either. Talbott was a camera without an artist's mind behind it. You want ten-thousand pictures of a pigeon couchant, we've got them. So Irma can stop sweating a little. They're worth nothing, maybe a buck apiece as a mail-order curiosity. Of course, you've got to convince the IRS of this, so the lawyer's fees will take a bit off the inheritance."

"Mr. Gold, if the sketches are worthless, how can they be a motive for murder?" asked Warshafsky.

"If Irma thought they were worth three billion, they were her motive. She would have a hard time convincing a jury of working slobs that she did it all for love. Now try this: Six months ago, when Irma and Erik decided to get married, she wanted to check one thing. She's really a simple girl at heart, not like the jet setters she thought she had to imitate. She wanted a baby, and right now, because she was already pushing thirty-five. So Erik got a general checkup and a fertility test; count, motility, everything. He passed with flying colors. Also a blood test, Rh factor and all. They were highly compatible, babywise. It's on the record. Erik used the company's medical insurance. Mistake, although I would have found out anyway. Cheap is cheap, Erik."

"You have copies?" asked Warshafsky. "Give them to me." He was beginning to sound interested.

"My wife and her able assistant have files full of everything for you. Real evidence."

"Good, I'll send an officer to pick it up. We'll dig along the lines you suggested, Mr. Gold, and see what we can turn up. You've been helpful but, as an amateur, you don't realize what we need to go to a Grand Jury. You have no evidence that Kirsch was the perpetrator; you can't even put him in the house at the time. There may be enough to hold Mrs. Talbott, at least as a material witness," Irma burst into tears again, "which I will discuss with the D.A. today. Meanwhile," he turned to the architects, "none of you are to leave this jurisdiction without checking with me." He rose to leave.

XXIV

"Sit down, Lieutenant," said Alexander, "and this amateur will give you some real evidence. How would you like to have a deathbed statement from the deceased?"

"You have that, Gold? It is illegal to withhold evidence from the police. You are required to turn it over to me at once."

"You have it, Lieutenant, look in your files. Surely you have a copy of Talbott's last masterpiece?"

"We have."

"Did you notice the doodles in the lower left-hand corner?"

"I studied them carefully for hours."

"I saw them for about a minute. Here's what they say. Remember, Talbott had only a minute to name his killer, and couldn't do it in an obvious way. But it's there. The radish and the sausage? They're really a radish and a sausage. Talbott was very literal, he could only draw what he had seen. That's the famous Munich second breakfast, the one that every *Münchner Kindl* eats religiously every day: *Weisswurst und Radi.* Munich white-veal sausage and the giant Bavarian white radish. Munich, where Erik and Irma started the whole thing.

"Next, the section of the roof. It really is a roof section, one that is pretty much standard today. You see—" he stopped and pointed to Kirsch, "Look at that face, Lieutenant, he's suddenly realized what he missed in the heat of getting out of the studio." Erik smiled again, calmly.

Warshafsky motioned to Alexander to go on. "A common flat-slab roof has insulation applied on top of the concrete slab, several piles of roofing membrane laid over the insulation, and crushed stone or slag over the roofing to protect it from sun and physical damage. A newer kind of roof has the roof membranes right on the concrete, with the insulation over the roofing and the crushed stone over the insulation, just as in Talbott's doodle. The advantage is better protection for the roof membranes against drying, physical damage, and thermal shock.

"Now you may wonder why Talbott, who never used a roof in his life, much less a flat roof like this, should draw this section. The building he was working on had no flat roof surfaces. This kind of roof is not suitable for steeply pitched roofs, but it is highly suitable for giving information. The roof is called 'Insulated Roof Membrane Assembly.' I-R-M-A. The Irma Roof. You like that, Lieutenant?"

"I like it. What's doodle number three?"

"Oh that's just the most famous church in Munich. In English, The Church of the Lady, or The Church of the Madonna. Some say the name comes from the two rounded spires, that the spherical tops represent breasts, but that's not true. The German name is *Frauenkirche.* To an American with no ear for the subtleties of language, it could easily sound like *Frau und Kirsch,* wife and Kirsch. Finished."

Warshafsky was silent, thinking. One of the insurance

men turned to the other and said, "I don't care what the police do, it will be a cold day in hell before Mrs. Talbott or any member of Talbott Associates sees one penny from any of our policies." The other man merely nodded.

Alexander sighed, picked up the paper bag from his desk, and slowly began removing the sealing tape. "The trouble is, Irma has been spending her husband's money even faster than he made it, buying her way into the jet set. And your bank account, Erik, is empty, too. God knows where you stashed the money, you certainly didn't spend it, but I'll bet it's where you can't get at it easily from this jurisdiction, even if they let you out on bail. Naturally, no one will hire Talbott Associates to do a doghouse from now on if you are still associated with it. I think you've made your associates very unhappy." Kirsch glanced uneasily at them, lingering on Bishop's impassive face.

"If I were R.C. I might even have someone quietly get rid of you, for his daughter's sake, if nothing else. Dakin and Bauer? I'd hate to be in the same city as either of them when they fully realize how you've ruined them. As for John Bishop, what you have done to him is somewhat more severe than blowing smoke in to his face." Kirsch looked even more uneasy. Bishop smiled at him sweetly, the same sweet smile as when he told us how he would like to watch his victim's eyes when he killed him.

"Think, Erik, have you really covered all your tracks perfectly? The clerk who sold you the knife, would you bet your life she wouldn't remember you? Because that's what you're doing, betting your life. The police will dig into your life, Erik. They may be slow but they are very thorough.

"The D.A. may not have a watertight case against you, Erik, you were too careful for that. But your friend Irma, she is vulnerable. It really wasn't gentlemanly to leave her holding the bag. She may resent that, a bit, may even feel a little betrayed. Will she talk? R.C. and her lawyer will explain the facts of life to her: If she keeps her mouth shut, you get off, and she goes away for a long, long time. If she makes a deal with the D.A., she gets off easy, maybe with only probation. After all, she was the accessory, you stuck in the knife. You think she won't talk? Erik, she will sing like a little birdy, tweet, tweet, tweet. Does she love you so much that she would give up her life for you? Are you sure? Would you, for her?"

As Alexander was talking, R.C. turned and looked directly at Burton. Burton lifted one eyebrow slightly. R.C. moved his head up and down one-half inch. Burton nodded one-eighth inch. The deal was made, the contract sealed. Erik watched the little drama, his smile gone. His body no longer relaxed, he turned back to Alexander.

Alexander opened the paper bag. "But cheer up, Erik. Irma brought you a present. She wants to make sure you design exactly the same way that Roger Talbott did. Here is a square." Alexander threw a small block, underhand, at Kirsch. It landed in his lap.

"And here is a cube." Alexander threw another block, overhand, hitting Kirsch in the chest. "And here is a rectangle." Alexander hit him in the face with it. "And my-oh-my, what have we here? Why it's a darling little pyramid." Alexander hit him in the face again, harder. "And another pyramid, lucky you." Again, in the face, hard. "And another pyramid; you'll be able to design great buildings with these, Erik." In the face. And another, and another, and another, each time in the face, each time harder than the last, "And another pyramid, and another pyramid, and one more pyramid, and another—"

Suddenly Kirsch stood up and drew a tiny double-barreled gun from his sweatpants. "Put it on the floor, Lieutenant," he said. "Two fingers, gently. Push it under the chair with your foot, all the way." Warshafsky pushed his gun under the chair.

Kirsch pointed his gun at Alexander. "It's a derringer, Mr. Gold. Small but deadly at close range. Magnum cartridges. Smooth bore, so the bullets tumble a little. Makes a bigger hole inside than you might guess. I'm leaving now, going to where my money is. I didn't think it would happen this way, but I'm a planner. I covered all the eventualities, the way I did with Roger. That's why I wore the sweatsuit today. You knew, didn't you, Mr. Gold."

"I knew, but I though you would break long ago. Go then, no one will stop you."

"Sure they will, at the airport. Everything is ready there, but they'll stop me. So I'm taking Mrs. Gold along. I'll turn her loose when I get to where I'm safe." He pointed the gun at me.

Alexander shook his head. "That was a mistake, Erik. Please turn the gun back on me." Kirsch didn't move. Alexander said, quietly, "I am going to stand up, so it would be sensible for you to turn the gun on me." Kirsch still kept the gun pointed at my chest. Alexander stood up. I noticed that he put both his feet to the left of his chair. I've learned to watch him carefully.

"I'm taking my shirt off, Erik. Point the gun at me." Alexander slowly took off his shirt.

"Look at this, Erik," Alexander said. He spread his legs by stepping left, and flexed his arms in the classical strongman's pose. "Did you ever see such huge muscles, Erik?" he asked. The diet had taken off some of Alexander's subcutaneous fat, leaving every muscle cut sharp and clear. I have never seen him look so big, so powerful, so overwhelming.

Alexander swiveled around one hundred and eighty degrees on his left foot and said, "Back pose. Great, huh?" He spread his back muscles, his huge lats like full sails. "Side pose," he called, swiveling on his right foot and inflating his chest, pectorals like two horizontal melon halves. I could see what he was doing and I wanted to scream 'no, no, don't, me,' but I didn't interfere, I didn't want the gun pointed at him. I grabbed my notebook in my right hand and got ready.

Alexander turned once more, facing Kirsch, who was watching in fascinated disbelief. "Turn the gun on me, Erik, please." That was Alexander's soft, sweet reasonable voice. Kirsch didn't know what it meant.

Alexander spoke quietly, soothingly. "Erik, shortly after I got married, when I was still overwhelmed with the wonder of having Norma as my wife, I told her that if it ever came to it, I would give my life for her. She didn't believe me, I think, but that's how I felt then and that's how I feel now, even more strongly. Please point the gun at me.

"No? Well I would, of course, try to avoid a situation where it became necessary, but when it is unavoidable, as it seems to be now, I will die for her. So I ask again, for the last time, point the gun at me."

Kirsch did not.

Alexander stepped left and flexed his arms again. "Look at this, Erik. Huge, Powerful. I am as strong as I look. I am not going to let my wife go with you so you can kill her in safety. I can't even stop you from shooting at her now. But I promise you, if you shoot at her, even if you miss, I will put one foot on each of your shoulders and tear your head off. Tear your head off, Erik, do you understand? Pull it right off, Erik! Rip it off, Erik! Blood, Erik! Your blood, Erik, gushing out all over the floor! And there's no way you can stop me. Even if you shoot me in the heart with the second bullet, I will live enough seconds to tear your head off. I am only six feet from you now, Erik. I can reach you in half a second. Decide! Do you want to take your chance in court? Do you want to kill me? Or do you really want to shoot my wife and have me pull your head off? Decide!" Alexander's voice cracked like a whip.

I got ready. Kirsch glanced from Alexander to me to Alexander and back to me. His finger tightened on the trigger, his arm lifted a fraction of an inch, and he began to swing the gun toward Alexander. He was going to kill my poor, sick, wounded husband.

"Me! Me!" I screamed, and threw my steno pad at him. He fired, the gun flashing toward the fluttering pages. At the same time Alexander's left hand lashed out with that incredible speed of his. He caught Kirsch's forearm in that tremendous grip, pushing down and angling up at the same time; you could hear the bones crack across the room. With his right hand he slapped Kirsch across the side of the head with a hard flat palm. Kirsch's head snapped sideways and he crumpled.

Alexander turned to me with a worried look. I suddenly felt dizzy and wet and warm and cold; I had been hit and didn't even know it. It didn't matter, I had my husband, my real husband, my live husband, back again.

"You lied to me again, Alexander," I said as the nurse went to get a vase for the flowers. Where do you get lilies-of-the-valley in October? "You said you would kill him if he shot at me. I saw you. You purposely hit him gently."

"I know," he looked miserable. "I was thinking of the money. The deals were for arrest and conviction. You can't convict a dead man."

"How could you think about money when someone is trying to kill your fantastic wife?"

"Only with a small part of my mind. I had the situation under control. I was inching over so I would be between the gun and you; then I would have had him. If you hadn't thrown the book— It was all your fault."

"Typical filthy little beast, blaming your wife for everything. All glands and no brains. Maybe I didn't want him to shoot you, did that ever cross your pointy head?"

"You wanted him to shoot you instead, you moron? That's biologically unsound; the male is supposed to—"

"Shut up," I broke in. "You owe me one and you know

it. A big one. And I don't want any arguments, either."

"All right," he grudged, "I owe you a big one."

"Good," I gloated. "Now repeat after me, 'I, Alexander Magnus Gold, husband third grade, maybe less, hereby promise my terrific wife, Norma, on her bed of pain caused by my rottenness and stupidity, that—"

"Wait," he jumped, "I know what you're going to say, and if you really want that, I'll do it. But can I please say something first?"

I nodded, what could I lose? He leaned over and took both of my hands in his, concerned and tender, and it was only maybe half put on. Not even half; score it one hundred percent concerned and fifty percent tender. "Norma," he said, "please don't ask me to give up detective work. It's socially useful. I'm good at it, it pays well, I can do it from the house, and it helps people."

"And it's fun for you," I added.

"Well, yes, that too," he admitted. That too? Hah! That's It, the rest is filler.

"You mean you have the incredible nerve to want another favor from me?" I asked incredulously. "When you haven't even started to pay off the first? You want to owe me *two* big ones?"

"Yes, please, terrific wife, please." Begging yet!

"Okay. For you I'll do it, but it will spoil my day."

"Thank you, terrific wife. I owe you two big ones."

Suddenly I felt weak and leaned back against the pillow. "I think I'll wait. I'm a little tired now." He looked at me, worried. If I played my cards right I could keep him being nice for two full weeks. Maybe more. Also he owed me two wishes. Big ones. Trying to figure out what they could be, and the suspense of waiting for my announcement, would be the punishment he so richly deserved for worrying me like that with his stupid heart attack. If the big ape had been able to keep his big mouth shut for a lousy thirty seconds more, the score would have been zero. At the proper time, when it will kill him the most, I'm going to tell him what my first big wish would have been: that what I really wanted, more than anything in the world, was to keep on working with him as a team, detecting.